HOW KIRSTY Jenkins STOLE THE ELEPHANT

HOW KIRSTY Jenkins STOLE THE ELEPHANT

ELEN CALDECOTT

BLOOMSBURY
LONDON NEW DELHI NEW YORK SYDNEY

Bloomsbury Publishing, London, New Delhi, New York and Sydney

First published in Great Britain in January 2009 by Bloomsbury Publishing Plc
50 Bedford Square, London WC1B 3DP

www.bloomsbury.com

A CIP catalogue record for this book is available from the British Library

ISBN 978 0 7475 9919 7

Typeset by Dorchester Typesetting Group Ltd
Printed and bound in Great Britain by CPI Group (UK) Ltd, Croydon CR0 4YY

13

For my siblings
And, of course, Simon

SUMMER

CHAPTER 1

Kirsty stumbled and fell towards the acid-green leaves. As they scratched her face she realised that they were exactly the same colour as the Amazonian poisonous frogs she had seen in the river earlier. She got back to her feet quickly. This was a dangerous place; deadly snakes hunted in the canopy above, jaguars padded through the undergrowth. She stepped forwards carefully so that the ginormous, man-eating beetles couldn't gnaw her boots. One of her fellow explorers had lost his big toe that way only yesterday. Her stomach rumbled. She had been trekking for days and supplies were running low.

'Can I eat some peas, Grandad?' she shouted.

The thump, thump of her grandad's shovel stopped.

'Are you still there? I thought you'd gone home,' said Grandad.

'No. I'm just on an expedition. We've got no food. We might have to resort to cannibalism. So, can I eat some of the peas? Please, please?' Her fingers came to rest on a thick pod right above her left shoulder. She grinned at Grandad, even though she couldn't see him past the wigwam of leaves.

'You're worse than all the birds, slugs and snails put together. I'm amazed I ever have anything to take home from this allotment.' Grandad started shovelling again. 'Go on, then. I wouldn't want you to have to eat any fellow explorers.' Kirsty heard him chuckle.

The pod cracked open between her thumbs. Her tongue teased out each pea and guided it on to her back teeth. Then, *crunch*, her whole mouth flooded with sweetness. She settled down on to her back, looking up through the leaves at the summer-bright sky. Grandad was digging again. She could hear noises on the other plots too: the squeak of a wheelbarrow, the whistle of a kettle boiling on a gas stove, shouts and laughter as people gave each other advice. Everyone was here today, working on their little plot of land. They all grew fruit and vegetables to take home. But none of them did it as well as Grandad. She picked a wodge of chewed pea off her back tooth. If only she could eat Grandad's peas every day! When she ruled the world it would always be summer and peas would grow all the time. And she wouldn't have to share a room with Dawn every weekend, bossing everyone around just because she was the eldest.

Thinking about Dawn made her feel annoyed. She sat up quickly and the leaves scratched her face again. The expedition! She had almost forgotten! Kirsty clapped her hands. Her fellow explorers leapt to attention. She had managed to find them food, scavenged from the unwilling jungle. That would stop the whispers of mutiny. For now. She uncurled the ancient map of Hazdrubal and set a course south. She was either leading them to untold riches, or to certain death. Only time would tell which it was to be. With one hand holding her compass and the other clutching a knife, Kirsty hacked a path through the clinging vines.

'Come on, pet.' The shovelling had stopped. Grandad was just outside her pea wigwam.

'It isn't time to go,' Kirsty said.

'I'm afraid it is. I promised your dad I'd have you home early today. It's the weekend. Ben and Dawn will be at your house soon. You never know, you might even have fun with your brother and sister.'

'Half-sister,' Kirsty muttered. Dad was Ben and Dawn's dad too, but they had a different mum. Dad had been married to their mum once, but then he had married Kirsty's mum. At weekends they came to Kirsty's house. Ben was nice, but Dawn was a total pain. When she wasn't there, Kirsty and Dad would do nice things together, like listen to Dad's records or watch Kirsty's DVDs, or even just rearrange their collections. But when Dawn was there, she moaned and yelled and spoiled everything.

Kirsty curled up inside the plants. It was a tight squeeze, though she knew that Grandad had planted them wide apart just so she could keep on using her den. She rested her head on the ground. It smelled of warm earth and the tang of leaves. A few weeds had grown up among the peas. She pulled one out of the ground, its silvery roots and all.

'If you don't come out, I'll have to come in and get you!' Grandad said.

Kirsty started giggling despite herself. She knew what was coming. Grandad was going to get her to move the way he always did – with lots of laughing and screaming. His hand reached in and grabbed her bare foot. His rough fingertips tickled and tickled her sole until she cried with laughter.

'Stop it! Stop it!' she yelled. Now there would be a twisting tug-of-war as she tried to break free. She yanked her leg. Grandad's grip loosened. Her foot sprang back towards her. He had let go. Grandad had let go on the first tug! That wasn't right. Kirsty frowned.

Cough, cough, cough.

It sounded like Grandad was coughing from some place deep, deep inside. It sounded like it hurt. Kirsty struggled out through the plants.

'Grandad?'

He was bent over, coughing into his huge white handkerchief. At the sound of her voice, Grandad looked up. His eyes were all watery. 'I'm fine, pet. Right as rain.' But he struggled to get the words out.

Kirsty shivered, despite the sunlight.

WINTER

CHAPTER 2

Kirsty was already awake, even before the phone rang. She couldn't sleep. Grandad had been in hospital for ages. Summer had turned into autumn, and now winter was here and every week Grandad got worse. Today, at the end of visiting hours, the doctor had taken Dad aside and whispered to him. And then Dad had picked up Dawn and Ben from their mum's house and asked them to come and stay, even though it was a Monday and not the weekend at all.

It all seemed wrong, and scary.

And then the phone rang in the middle of the night. 'Waaake up, waaake up,' it seemed to say.

Suddenly, everyone was awake, as if they had just been pretending to sleep too. Mum came in and turned on the light and then she was gone. Dawn was out of bed, but with that angry-bear face that meant

11

you shouldn't speak to her. Kirsty went to the bedroom door. Dad was on the landing. Ben came out of the front room, where he slept, carrying his jeans.

Kirsty felt cold all over.

'What's going on?' she asked. Nobody answered. 'Mum?'

Mum came out of her bedroom. 'That was the hospital on the phone, love. They want us to get there as soon as we can. Please go and get dressed.'

The car park was almost empty when they got to the hospital. They all got out of the car. Kirsty's breath rose in white mists, like ghosts floating up into the sky.

Inside, the hospital smelled sad. It gave her a funny pain in her chest. Just past the front doors, Ben stopped. He stood still in the middle of the corridor. Kirsty suddenly felt sorry for him, even though he was three years older than her. His eyes were wide and shiny. His clothes were done up wrong. He seemed to be trembling. Dawn stood next to him, not moving. She looked cross and crumpled.

'Are you OK?' Mum asked.

Ben didn't speak.

'Are you . . . would you like your mum to be here?'

Mum said.

Ben nodded gratefully.

'There are some phones downstairs,' Mum said. 'Dawn will help you, won't you, love? Come up as soon as you're done.'

Upstairs, a nurse stepped out from an office as they passed by. 'Mr Jenkins?' he asked. Dad stopped. The nurse looked serious but kind. Mum put her hand on Dad's arm as the nurse talked.

Kirsty tried to listen to what the nurse said, but she couldn't concentrate. Grandad was what mattered. Getting to Grandad. The grown-ups were busy talking to each other. Kirsty looked down the corridor. It was empty. She knew which room was Grandad's. She took a few steps backwards, away from the adults. She pressed her back against the wall and moved towards Grandad's room. She opened the door.

'Grandad?'

He didn't move. She was too late. The pain in her chest throbbed hard.

'Grandad?'

His head turned slowly. 'Kirsty, pet? You're a sight for sore eyes.'

'Oh Grandad!' Kirsty rushed across the room and

dropped down on to the bed. She buried her face in the crisp hospital sheets. The tears felt hot in her eyes. Grandad's thin hand came to rest on the back of her head. It was so light! Small, small strokes that she could hardly even feel, as though he was fading away.

'Shh,' he whispered. 'Shh. Stop these tears. You're like a wet weekend in Blackpool, and I've had quite enough of those for one lifetime.'

Kirsty grinned despite herself. 'How are you, Grandad?'

'Not too bad. I've got all these machines to keep me right.' He lifted his hand towards the equipment that blinked and hummed around his bed. 'Listen, pet. I'm glad to see you. Right glad.'

Kirsty had to get right up close to hear what Grandad was saying. His voice was hardly even a whisper.

'Listen. What do you think about my allotment?'

'Your allotment?' Kirsty said.

'Yes. Do you like it?'

'Of course I do! It's brilliant. The best ever. It's the jungle, and it's Sherwood Forest, and it's that place in Harry Potter with the massive spiders.'

'The Forbidden Forest?'

'Yes. I love your allotment.' It was true. All her best games and adventures happened there.

'Good. Because I want you to look after it for me.'

'Why, where are you going?'

Grandad didn't answer. A machine bleeped a few times, then everything was silent again. Kirsty swallowed a sob.

'Will you do it? Will you look after it?' Grandad asked.

Kirsty nodded. She couldn't stop the tears now. 'I promise.'

FRIDAY

CHAPTER 3

A week after Grandad died, Kirsty sat on an upturned bucket at the Jubilee Street allotments. There was no one else there. It was too cold. Wind buffeted the few straggling plants, freezing the tears on her cheeks.

The allotment was hers now. She had made a promise and she was going to keep it.

Kirsty stood up. She looked at the frozen ground. She was going to take care of it, bring it back to life. Grandad had asked her to. Just now it was wintry and bare, but she would wake it up. It was her Narnia. She was like Lucy, bringing hope. She would make it special again! She would be the new queen! She wiped her cheeks – this was no time for a ruler to go to pieces. There were important decisions to make.

She turned around slowly to get a better view of her new kingdom. The shed was behind her. Last summer, she and Grandad had painted it a swirl of bright colours: a pair of dolphins leapt over a yin-yang symbol. The dolphins had been her idea, the yin-yang was Grandad's. He said it helped him concentrate when he did his yoga. In front of the shed, a narrow brick path led down between the beds to the compost bin and water butt at the end. There wasn't much growing in the beds. Somehow, it hadn't seemed right to do very much here with Grandad away. But now it was her allotment and she had hard work to do.

'In the spring, I'm going to plant you full of bulbs. Thousands of daffodils!' she said to an empty patch of dark soil. 'And in you,' she said to another, 'I'm going to grow giant sunflowers and huge daisies and ginormous poppies!'

She might have to grow a few vegetables too. Grandad would want that. His favourite had been marrows. Every now and then, when the marrows ripened, they would have the name of one of the family on the side. The names weren't carved out with a knife or painted on. They were just there, part of the marrow itself. The green skin would have a few yellow streaks, these streaks would grow together, spreading in thin fingers until they touched, and suddenly a name would appear. Grandad would smile and say they had been visited by fairies. Kirsty thought that Grandad did it, but she didn't know how to do it by herself. And anyway, she didn't like the taste of marrows; they were like dinosaur skin wrapped around snot. It would have to be something else. Peas! Huge ones the size of apples!

Her allotment was going to be the best ever. She would keep her promise. She would make it famous. People would come from miles around to see her forest of flowers. And the humongous peas. For a moment, the pain she had been feeling for so many days seemed to ease a little.

'Oi!'

Kirsty looked up.

'Oi! You!'

A man was walking towards her. He moved fast, waving a clipboard in the air as if he was trying to land a plane. He hurried across the allotments. He was out of breath when he reached her. His bright red face swelled out of his beige coat as though he were a giant matchstick.

'What are you doing here?' he asked.

Kirsty paused, then said, 'I'm planning my plot.'

'Well don't,' he said. 'This is private property.'

'I know it is. It belongs, I mean . . . it belonged to my grandad.'

The man seemed to shrink a little, like a balloon

three days after a birthday. He looked down. He shuffled his polished shoes against the uneven brick path.

'I'm sorry for your loss,' he mumbled.

'Thank you,' Kirsty said.

'You're welcome,' the man said. Then his skin flushed even redder. 'Only, it didn't belong to your grandad. He rented it from the council. Everyone here rents from the council. They don't own their plots. And now, well, the council are going to take it back.'

Kirsty frowned. 'I'm Kirsty Jenkins. Who are you?'

The man looked surprised.

'I'm Malcolm Thomas. I mean, Mr Thomas. I work for the council. I'm the Community Environmental Development Officer.' Mr Thomas seemed to swell a little again when he told her his title. He looked at his clipboard. 'The thing is, you see, there's a waiting list for these allotments. And now that your grandad has . . . passed on, it really has to go to someone else. On the list, I mean.'

'But it's going to me. I promised my grandad.'

Mr Thomas looked her up and down, then he shook his head.

'No it isn't.'

'But I promised.'

'No,' said Mr Thomas.

Kirsty sat back down on the bucket. She had a

22

hollow space inside, a cold pain in her tummy.

She looked up. Mr Thomas was wandering around the allotment, scribbling tiny notes to himself on the clipboard. He ignored her completely. She might have been just another stalk of sprouts as far as he was concerned. She wanted to plead with him, to beg him to change his mind. But somehow the words wouldn't come. She couldn't think properly. The raised lip on the bottom of the bucket was pressing into her leg, but she found that she couldn't move. She had to keep herself still and small until Mr Thomas went away. At last, Mr Thomas had finished ticking his clipboard. He slipped his pencil into the breast pocket of his coat. He walked past her, stopped and opened his mouth. No words came out. He coughed, then carried on walking. He was gone.

Kirsty stood up. The afternoon sky was beginning to darken. 'It's not fair,' Kirsty muttered. She scuffed her shoes along the path, kicking against the raised bricks. 'It's not fair,' she whispered to the leeks.

Kirsty ran home and found Mum in the front garden, filling her bird feeders. The feeders hung down all around the garden, dripping husks on to the grass and the two broken Ford Escorts.

'It's not fair!' Kirsty shouted.

'What's not fair?' Mum asked.

'Mr Thomas from the council says I can't have Grandad's allotment. He says it has to go to the next people on the stupid list.'

'What stupid list?'

'A stupid waiting list. Mum, what are we going to do?'

'Oh,' Mum frowned. 'Kirsty love, I'm sorry, but we aren't going to do anything. He's right. You can't take over the allotment.'

Kirsty stared at Mum. Her stomach seemed to flip inside her, as though the garden had suddenly plummeted down a lift. 'Why not?'

'Well. You just can't. You're too young. Besides, it's dangerous to go down there on your own. There's all those strangers and sharp tools and germs and tetanus in the soil.'

'But, Mum, Grandad asked me to! I want to!'

'And the council says no. There are a hundred reasons.'

'Not real reasons. I made a promise.'

'Grandad wasn't thinking straight by the end. If he was, he would never have asked you.'

'There was nothing wrong with Grandad – until he died!' Kirsty shouted.

'Kirsty, please. Don't yell.'

Kirsty turned away. Dad was standing at an upstairs window, looking down at them. Dad would help! He'd understand! Kirsty lifted her hand and waved. Dad didn't move. It was as though he couldn't see her.

'Dad?' Kirsty whispered.

'He's gone to lie down. He's tired,' Mum said, still busy with the feeders.

Kirsty waved again.

Dad turned slowly away from the window. He was gone.

SATURDAY

CHAPTER 4

It almost felt like Ben and Dawn had moved in. They had stayed last weekend, then on Monday night, then again for the funeral and now it was the weekend and they were here *again*. Kirsty stood outside her bedroom door, her palm resting on the wood. Dawn was inside unpacking, which just meant that she was moving all of Kirsty's stuff and spreading her own stuff everywhere instead. Kirsty took a deep breath and then opened the door.

'Out!' Dawn yelled. She was sitting on the floor, surrounded by clothes and her sketchbook. Her mobile phone was clamped to her ear. Kirsty was sure that Dawn only spent so much time on her mobile to show off. Kirsty wasn't allowed one, as her Mum didn't like them.

'It's my room! I can come in if I want.' Kirsty took

a step forward.

Dawn's eyes flashed devil red. She grabbed the nearest thing and threw it at Kirsty. Luckily, the nearest thing was a woolly jumper. Kirsty stepped back as a marker pen followed the jumper. She skipped out of the room and closed the door. This was unbelievable! Just yesterday she had been Queen Kirsty, ruler of her own kingdom. Today she'd been bullied out of her own bedroom. This wasn't supposed to happen to royalty. They could do whatever they wanted to whoever they wanted. Oh for a cauldron of boiling oil over the door to stop Dawn getting in. Or catapults around the house to stop Dawn getting through the front gate. Or a band of loyal knights to stop Dawn ever coming down the street! Kirsty kicked the door with the back of her heel. Then she went to see what Ben was doing.

He was where he usually was, in the front garden, sitting behind the wheel of the red Ford Escort. The car had piles of bricks where its wheels were meant to be and no engine. The other car in the front garden had wheels, but it was painted grey and who'd ever heard of a grey racing car? So Ben always drove the red car. One day Dad was going to make one working car out of the two broken ones, but that hadn't happened yet. Kirsty could hear other people playing in the street, the clatter and fall of boys on skateboards, but Ben was louder than any of them.

'And he accelerates up past the pack, he overtakes the lead car, taking the turn on the inside – this is the fastest time this course has ever seen,' Ben yelled. He pulled hard on the wheel, braking around the corner. He let out a piercing shriek as the car nearly spun out of control.

Kirsty opened the passenger door and got in.

'The crowd is going wild. Surely this is the best performance they've seen since Schumacher retired. Jenkins is way ahead of the other drivers and still accelerating.'

'Ben?'

Ben slammed on the brakes. The car skidded, then shuddered to a halt. The crowd fell silent. 'What?'

'What would you do if you wanted something really badly and everyone said you couldn't have it?'

'Dunno. Moan, whine? Why, what's going on?'

'Mum and the council say that I can't look after Grandad's allotment. But I can, I know I can. How do I make them change their mind?'

'I dunno . . . Can you just pester them about it? You're good at that.'

'That might work on Mum and Dad, but it isn't going to work on the council man, is it?'

'I suppose not. I don't get it. Why aren't you allowed?'

'I'm too young. It's dangerous for me to be out by myself. I'll put a spade through my foot and bleed to death with no one around to call an ambulance.'

'Your Mum said that?'

'Yes. Almost. And the council have a waiting list. People queuing for allotments! The stupid council man says Grandad's bit has to go to the next person on the stupid waiting list. What Grandad said doesn't matter to them.' Kirsty took a deep breath, then said quietly, 'Grandad asked me to look after it, see. When he was at the hospital. I promised him I would.'

'Oh.' Ben popped the gear stick into first gear and growled as he restarted the engine. Kirsty stared at him.

'Ben? Aren't you going to help me?'

'I dunno. Don't you think it's weird that Dad hasn't got out of bed today?'

'You're changing the subject.'

'Yes, but don't you think it's weird?'

'Mum said he was tired.'

'He can't stay in bed all day though.'

'Perhaps he feels poorly. Ben, listen to me. It can't go to strangers. I promised.'

'What can't?'

'The allotment. Concentrate. They'll paint his shed brown and plant boring stuff in neat rows. There won't be marrows with names on, I bet!'

'You don't even like marrows.'

'That's not the point! If someone else takes over, they'll make it all ordinary. And soon you won't be able to tell which allotment was Grandad's. He'll be gone for good.'

'Kirsty, he is gone.'

'No he isn't, not if we keep the garden alive. Keep it special. He won't be properly gone. And it will be nice for Dad too, won't it? When he feels better he can come and help us look after it.'

Ben was quiet for a minute, his hands resting on the the steering wheel, just like Dad's did when he was driving. Then he looked at Kirsty. 'OK, I'll help. What do you want me to do?'

Kirsty smiled widely at him. Ben was brilliant! 'How do grown-ups get what they want?' she asked.

'Demonstrations, petitions, they write to the prime minister, they picket and they go on telly. Like Grandad did about the war. Some people climb up trees and live there for ages. That might be fun, like being Robin Hood.'

'That's brilliant! Should we do all of those things?'

'I wouldn't mind doing the tree one.'

33

'There aren't any trees at the allotment, but there's the shed. We could live in that for a bit?'

Ben pulled a face. 'It's got spiders in it. Anyway, before we try the other stuff perhaps you should go and talk to the council man first? You never know, he might be nice.'

Kirsty thought about Mr Thomas's red face and shiny shoes. 'I don't think he will be,' she said, 'but I suppose we should try.'

MONDAY

CHAPTER 5

On Monday, after school, Ben and Kirsty met outside the council buildings.

'This is exciting!' Kirsty said. 'Like a spy mission.'

Ben grinned. 'Yes. We should hide. Do some surveillance.'

'Cool. In there.' Kirsty pointed towards a phone box opposite the main doors. It was a tiny space, with just enough room for the phone, a small ledge and the two of them wedged one on top of the other. It smelled bad. Kirsty shoved Ben's arm out of the way so she could get a clear view of the staff leaving. The men were wrapped up in woolly coats, scarves muffling their heads. The women looked exactly the same but smaller.

'You'll never recognise him,' Ben said.

'Yes I will. His image is burned into my brain for

ever. He's the one that looks like a matchstick.'

The crowd thinned; some staff unchained their bikes and sped off in Day-Glo jackets; trams pulled up and whisked others away. Soon there was hardly anyone else left.

'We've missed him,' Ben said.

'No, no, there he is!'

Mr Thomas strolled down the stone steps, his umbrella clipping the edge of each one with a satisfying thwack. He smiled as the crisp winter air hit his cheeks. His face was as rosy red as ever.

'Come on,' Kirsty said. She pushed open the door.

Ben grabbed her arm. 'Not so fast. Don't you know anything about spying? He's our target, but we don't know anything about him. What makes him tick? If you want something from someone you have to ask in the right way.'

Kirsty grinned, then nodded. 'I know. Like, if I wanted some money from Mum, I'd tell her how important it is for my future. If I wanted money from Dad, I'd tell him that Mum says it's OK.'

'Exactly. We need Mr Thomas to change his mind, but we haven't got a clue about what will make him do that.'

Kirsty rolled her eyes. 'Well, 007, you'd best be quick. He's leaving.'

Ben nodded, then raised a finger to his lips. He crouched low and pushed open the door. Kirsty dropped down behind him. They were a commando unit, silent, deadly, with a licence to kill. Ben ran forwards, bent double. He stopped behind a postbox. He peered around it, a short, decisive glance, just to keep Mr Thomas in view. Then he tapped the air with two fingers of his left hand: *move out*. Kirsty obeyed, running behind him, silent as an assassin. They kept to the shadows, hid behind lamp posts, slinked through crowds – always keeping Mr Thomas in view. He led them through the Old Town, down dark alleyways. Ben and Kirsty kept out of sight, but never lost their target.

Mr Thomas turned left down one of the closes. It was a narrow lane, still cobbled, not tarmacked. It was a short cut through to Cathedral Square.

'He's going to church!' Kirsty hissed.

'Perhaps. The museum is down here too. Or he might live in one of those funny old buildings next to the cathedral.'

Mr Thomas was swinging his umbrella now. They could hear him whistling as he walked. He glanced up at the stone monsters that swarmed over the west front of the cathedral, but he carried on past. When he reached the museum he practically skipped up the worn steps, passed the thick columns and then disappeared inside. Kirsty was ready to chase him, but Ben grabbed her arm again.

'Hold up, 006. We need to debrief, to look at our intelligence. What have you discovered about our target?'

Kirsty thought hard. 'Well, sir. He's gone to the museum. He likes whistling.'

'Is that it?' Ben was smiling now. 'We've learned loads. For example, think about his beige coat. Bit strange for a gardener. Beige isn't very practical. Grandad always wore his manky, old clothes. And did you see the way he was smiling when he came out of work? It was like he'd been given his freedom. I don't think that Mr Thomas likes gardening. I don't think he likes his job at all. Also, look at where he goes to relax – the museum! Mr Thomas likes culture. Did you hear *what* he was whistling?'

Kirsty frowned. 'No.'

'Oh dear, 006. That was a violin concerto by Vivaldi.'

'You what?'

'My mum plays it in her salon when she does manicures. Mr Thomas might look like a matchstick, but inside he's posh. He won't like being harassed by a lout. You're going to have to be polite. Sweet, even. Do you think you can do that?'

'Thould I have a lithp?'

'No. That's too much. Just be sweet and nice.'

'OK.'

'It's best you go alone, so he doesn't feel bullied. I'll wait for you out here. Are you ready to go and whine at him?'

'Ready as I'll ever be, 007.'

CHAPTER 6

Kirsty stepped into the main hall of the museum. It was all white marble and high ceilings. She had been here before, on one of their weekend family outings. They had had iced buns in the cafe. The stuffed elephant was cool; the mummies were a bit scary, but it had been fun.

In the middle of the hall was a woman in uniform sitting behind a desk. The desk was covered in leaflet holders. Adverts for steam trains and factory tours spilled on to the marble surface. Kirsty went up to the desk, smiling.

The woman in uniform leaned forwards to see Kirsty better. 'Hello. Can I help?'

'Yes, I'm looking for, erm, my uncle. He just came in. Did you see where he went? He's sort of tall, with a light brown coat on. His face is a bit red.'

The woman nodded. 'You mean Mr Thomas? From the board? Well, he usually goes to Natural History. He loves that. But today, I think I saw him go to Ancient Rome. Top of those stairs.' The woman pointed to a grand sweeping staircase behind the desk.

'Thank you very much,' Kirsty said. Polite, polite – she must remember to be polite. The stairs were beautiful; bright metal poles held a thick red carpet in place all the way up them. Her arm slid easily up the wooden handrail, as though it had been greased. This would be the perfect palace for a queen!

Her footsteps made no sound on the carpet. At the top of the stairs, she turned into the Roman gallery. There were objects in glass cases balanced on top of pillars. The only light in the room came from the small spotlights pointing to the objects. It was as though they were floating in the dark space. She could make out jugs and bottles, plates, bowls and roof tiles, the odd piece of dark twisted metal that could be anything at all. It was nothing like the Rome she had seen in films! The only other person in the room was Mr Thomas. He had his back to her.

Kirsty went to stand next to him and, as she did so, she watched his face reflected in the glass case. He was smiling slightly; he looked content. Then he caught sight of her reflection. He frowned but didn't turn around. Kirsty smiled as sweetly as she could manage. He ignored her.

'Hello,' she said brightly.

He turned a little and his eyes flicked towards her, but he didn't speak.

'Hello, Mr Thomas. Do you remember me?'

He turned to look at her properly. 'No,' he said and turned back to the case.

Kirsty looked up at him. The thick wool of his coat seemed to be like a shield around his thick body. She felt a lick of anger rise inside her. She squished it down; anger wasn't sweet.

'We met on Friday, er, sir. At my grandad's allotment. I was thinking about all the pretty flowers I want, I mean, I *would like* to grow. Don't you remember?'

'No.'

That was ridiculous! It was only three days ago!

'You must remember! You said I couldn't look after it!' Her voice sounded too loud in the dead space of the museum.

Mr Thomas turned to her with his eyebrows creased as though he were in pain. 'Shh! You can't shout in here. Where are your parents? You can't be here by yourself. There are rules.'

'There's no sign or anything. I can talk if I want.'

'Not to me, you can't. I said everything that there was to say last week.'

Kirsty bit her lip. *Be polite, be polite, be polite*, she repeated in her head. She took a deep breath. 'Please, Mr Thomas, I just want you to listen to me, just for a bit. Then I'll leave you alone. I want to keep the allotment and I think you should let me.'

Mr Thomas looked stunned; it was as though one of the jugs in the case behind him had started talking. Then he said, 'Do you see my desk here? My filing cabinet? My hole punch and stapler? No, you do not. Because I am not at work. This is my leisure time. Which I spend at leisure. Not talking to little girls. Your grandfather's allotment is vacant. I will write up the findings of my inspection this week and next week I will offer it to new tenants. End of story. Now, go away.'

Kirsty felt her hold on her temper loosen; it seemed to rise up out of her like the bubbles rushing out of a can of lemonade. He was going to give away the allotment next week! 'It's not fair. You won't even listen. It's not *fair*. I promised Grandad, and you won't even let me try. You don't care about anyone. Not me, or Grandad. All you care about is stupid old jugs and plates and . . . and . . . Vivaldi!'

'How did you . . . Have you been spying on me?'

Kirsty hung her head. 'No, not really, hardly at all.'

Mr Thomas's face turned a violent shade of purple, like plum jam smeared over a red postbox. 'What?' he roared. 'You've been following me? How dare you! You are a very rude little girl. Now, get out, go! If you ever come bothering me again. I'll call the police.'

'But, I just –'

'Out!'

Kirsty turned and ran.

CHAPTER 7

Kirsty rushed down the museum steps towards Ben. How dare Mr Thomas! He was stupid, grumpy and rude. She glared at Ben, then pulled tongues at the museum.

'Pester power didn't work, then?' Ben asked as Kirsty stomped up to him.

She shook her head.

'Oh.'

They started walking away from the museum. Kirsty swung her arms like a soldier. As she walked, her anger began to turn into something else. Determination.

'What was the first thing on your list, Ben? The way grown-ups get people to change their minds?'

'Demonstrations. You make banners and stand in the street.'

'Then that's what we'll do next.'

Ben stopped walking. He stood winding the hem of his jumper around his finger. He looked uncomfortable.

'What?' Kirsty asked.

He stared down at his twisted hem. 'Well. I dunno if it's a good idea. I dunno if I want to stand in the street. My mum might see, or Dad. They might be angry. We might get into trouble.'

'Dad won't see you. He didn't come out of his bedroom all weekend.' Kirsty felt a sudden shock as she said this. It was true; Dad hadn't come out of his room for ages. She frowned. That didn't seem right. Usually at weekends he'd be in the middle of all the noise and action. In fact, he would be making most of the noise, playing music, laughing, teasing everyone. But this weekend he'd been quiet, spending it alone in his room. It was weird. And Mum had cancelled his work this week. And *that* was weird because Dad never let people down; if he said he'd fit your kitchen by Friday, then it was done by Friday. Kirsty put her hand on Ben's arm and gave it a small squeeze. 'I'm sure it will be all right,' she said, though she didn't feel sure at all.

Ben let go of his jumper. 'Where would you want to have the demonstration?' he asked.

'The allotments? The council building? Which do

you think?'

'I think the council building would be best. Where Mr Thomas will see us.'

'Yes! He just said to me that I wasn't to bother him outside work. So I should bother him in work! I'm going to go home to paint a banner. Do you want to come?'

'No, I should go to my house. It's getting late. I'll make a banner there. I'll meet you outside the council building after school tomorrow.'

TUESDAY

CHAPTER 8

Kirsty's banner was beautiful. She had spent hours on Monday evening painting and gluing and glittering and now it was glorious. Two dolphins leapt over a silver, glittery yin-yang. They had huge smiles and speech bubbles coming out of their mouths. They were saying 'Give Kirsty Grandad's Alotmant'. She wasn't too sure of the spelling, but she didn't want to ask Mum in case it Aroused Suspicion. The banner was glued between two sticks, so that she could hold it up above her head.

Ben was already waiting when she got to the council building. He shuffled slowly towards her, holding a rolled-up something in his hand. She skipped over to him, her whole body fizzing with excitement.

'How should we do this?' he mumbled.

Kirsty looked about. It was still pretty cold and the few people in the street were huddled into their scarves and hats. A tram pulled past, its wheels clattering noisily over the rails. The council building behind them perched on top of a flight of concrete steps. It looked quite imposing all of a sudden.

'Well, I think we should go inside and uncurl our banners. And then we should shout something.'

'Yes, a slogan. Do we have a slogan?' Ben asked doubtfully.

'When Grandad went on the anti-war demonstration, he shouted rude things about the prime minister,' Kirsty said.

'Well, I don't think we should do that. It isn't the prime minister's fault, is it?'

'How about rude things about Mr Thomas?'

'No, you'll only upset him. How about, "Give us a garden!"? That sounds good.'

'Brilliant. Ready?'

Ben nodded slowly. Kirsty bounded up the steps, taking them two at a time. This was really exciting!

The council building was mostly green on the inside: moss green floor tiles, mint green walls, the odd cheese plant shrivelling in its pot. Even the chairs were a kind of mouldy green. The only other colour in the room was the red of the fire extinguishers mounted on the walls.

'Yuck,' Kirsty said.

'Like walking through snot,' Ben agreed.

'With a nosebleed.'

A few people stood in the foyer, but no one paid any attention to them. Beyond the foyer there was a lift and a set of stairs. A man sat at a desk next to the lift, but he didn't look up from his computer.

'This is great. Loads of room,' Kirsty said. 'Let's set up here.' She stood just to the left of the main entrance. A shower of glitter fell on her head as she uncurled the banner. Even better, now she was sparkly too. People were bound to pay attention. Ben uncurled his banner. It was brilliant! He had taken a black sheet and cut it in half; he'd stuck white letters on to it saying 'Allotments for Kids, Kids for Allotments'. All the letter 'l's were cut to look like shovels. *So that's how you spell it*, Kirsty thought. Never mind – hers was pretty close.

With their banners high in the air, Kirsty led the shout: 'Give us a garden! Give us a garden!' Ben shouted too, but a bit more quietly.

Their voices echoed around the foyer as though they were yelling down a well. The man at the computer looked up. Kirsty grinned at him and waved, but didn't stop shouting. He lifted a phone.

'Give us a garden! Give us a garden!' This was great.

Like proper protesters. This would make Mr Thomas listen. It had to. If only she'd brought a whistle, then they could make even more noise. A few people crossing the foyer stopped to stare. Some must work here; they had badges on strings around their necks. One or two were just ordinary people; they smiled at Kirsty. She smiled back. There was a little crowd gathering. This was brilliant!

'What on earth is going on here?' A man in a blue uniform stepped in front of their demonstration. He wasn't smiling like the other people.

Ben stopped shouting at once. Kirsty carried on, until Ben jabbed her painfully in the ribs.

The man still wasn't smiling. 'What do you two think you're doing?'

'It's a demonstration,' Kirsty said.

'I can see that,' the man said.

'We want Mr Thomas to change his mind and give me my grandad's allotment.'

Kirsty heard a woman in the crowd explaining to another who Mr Thomas was.

'And did you get permission for this display? From Security? From the relevant officers? From the local constabulary?' the man asked.

Kirsty shook her head. Ben let his banner droop to the ground.

'I thought not. This protest is illegal. You will have to stop immediately.'

A woman stepped forward from the crowd. 'They're not doing any harm. Let them be.'

Some people behind her gave small cheers of approval. The man in the uniform frowned. 'I can't do that. They're in violation of security codes.'

'They're just kids,' the woman said.

Kirsty felt a bit cross at that. She was a kid, but that didn't mean that she didn't have something important to say. Ben whispered in her ear, 'We should go.'

Kirsty shook her head and glared at him. She wasn't going anywhere, not until she had changed Mr Thomas's mind. 'Give us a garden! Give us a garden!' she yelled again, as loud as she could.

Some of the crowd started to cheer. The man in blue frowned at the crowd. Suddenly he reached out to grab Kirsty's banner. She stepped back, the poles angled away from him. *Crunch.* She felt the poles judder as they came up against something hard. Something breakable. She turned slowly. One of her poles was wedged squarely in the centre of a little red box, just above the fire extinguishers.

Wah, wah, wah, wah, wah.

The fire alarm was deafening. And she had set it off. She looked at the crowd, at the man in blue, at Ben, whose mouth hung open. It was like they were all frozen in time. Then she snapped to with a decision. 'Run!' she yelled.

They dropped the banners to the ground. She took Ben's hand and rushed towards the door. The man in blue made to grab at her, but she sidestepped past him. The whole building seemed to be shaking with the noise of the alarm. No, not the alarm. It was footsteps! The sound of hundreds of people tramping out of their offices, obeying the drill. She was going to be in such big trouble if they caught her!

She ran as fast as she could, out through the doors, down the steps, along the road, with Ben matching her step for step. She looked back once to see if they were being followed, but the man and the crowd seemed to have been caught up in the huge swell of people that were evacuating the council building. Hundreds of people spilled out on to the road. Kirsty and Ben dashed around the corner, running as though they had hell hounds chasing them. They swept past shops, pedestrians, tram stops, running as fast as they could. Somewhere behind them they could hear the wail of a fire engine.

It was only after four blocks that Ben slowed down. Kirsty grabbed her side where a stitch stabbed at her. She looked at Ben; he caught her eye. And then she felt the most delicious burst of laughter surge up out of her. She couldn't control it. She laughed so hard that she had to cling on to Ben to keep upright. Ben smirked, then chuckled and before long he was howling along with her.

'Did you see their faces?' Kirsty gasped.

'Brilliant.'

'And all those people getting out of work early.'

'Priceless. I can't believe you set off the alarm! That was crazy.'

'It was an accident. I didn't mean to!'

'It was genius.'

The giggles slowed now, occasionally just bubbling up in small spurts. They walked on slowly. Every now and again Kirsty remembered the man in the blue shirt, his eyes bulging out and his mouth sagging when he realised what she'd done. Then she had to snigger again.

'It was brilliant fun,' Ben said. 'But it didn't get us what we wanted.'

'No. Mr Thomas didn't even see it was us. We'll have to try another way. What else was on your list?'

'I don't think my list is very good. None of my sug-gestions have worked very well so far,' Ben said.

'It's not your fault. They were good ideas.'

'I dunno. Perhaps you should ask someone who's,

well, older.'

'Like who? My mum? Dad? They aren't going to help, are they?' Kirsty said.

'No. But Dawn might.'

'Dawn? She's the Wicked Witch of the West!' As she spoke, Kirsty imagined Dawn flying in every weekend on a broomstick, cackling at the clouds as they whipped past her.

Ben looked at Kirsty. 'I know she can be a pain at your place, but she's not always like that. Sometimes when it's just me and her she can be nice. I think she feels bad about . . . I mean, she's not always in a mood round our house. You should come home with me now and we can talk to her. She might help.'

'Yeah, and she might throw things at us until all that's left of us are two squishy piles of strawberry jam.'

Ben laughed and walked on. Kirsty followed him reluctantly. She couldn't believe that Dawn would ever agree to help. But who else was there to ask?

CHAPTER 9

Ben and Dawn's house, where they lived with their mum, was on the north side of town. They had to walk through the park and over the river to get there. Kirsty followed Ben across the twilit park. Neither of them spoke much. Kirsty's thoughts were whirling around, always coming back to the problem: what could they do next? Would Dawn help? Or would she just be her usual witchy self?

The sun had almost set by the time they reached the far side of the park. The sky was purple-blue. The trees looked black and gnarled, crouching in the thick shadows. Kirsty could hear strange rustling noises coming from the bushes. Actually, the park wasn't very nice at night. It was a bit creepy. The hairs on the back of Kirsty's neck bristled. And she was on her way to visit the Wicked Witch! She ran to keep up with Ben.

Ben let them into the house. Kirsty had never been into Ben's home, though she had waited outside in the car with Dad when he came to pick up Dawn and Ben. Dad would be so excited to see them, rabbiting on about it for the whole journey. But he wouldn't go in, because he didn't like talking to his ex-wife. So this was all new for Kirsty. Inside, it wasn't a witch's den at all; it was more like a fairy palace! Thick cream carpet stretched out in every direction; a complicated lamp-shade of twisted wire and gorgeous crystals shone light around the hallway; black-and-white-photographs of beautiful children marched up the staircase.

'Hey,' Kirsty laughed. 'It's you.' She pointed to a photo of a chubby toddler grinning sweetly at the camera.

'Shurrup,' Ben growled.

'So where's the witch?'

'She'll be in her room. We need to take up a cup of tea and a packet of chocolate digestives.'

'Cool. Talismans.'

'No, bribes. Come on.'

Ben moved around the kitchen arranging a tray of tea and biscuits. Kirsty just watched. She was too frightened to touch any of the beautiful shiny surfaces in case she made them dirty or broke something, although her fingers were itching to try the chrome juicer or the ice machine set into the fridge door. There must be a brilliant TV somewhere – one of those skinny ones that went on the wall, like having your own cinema. She'd love to have a go with it. Could she ask? No – she was here on a mission.

When he was done, Ben handed her the tray.

'You go up,' he said. 'She won't be expecting you. Element of surprise.'

'Which door?'

'It's the one with the sign that says, "Keep Out or I'll Feed You to My Piranhas".'

'Oh great.'

Kirsty took the stairs slowly, but the tea shook in its cup and sloshed on to the tray. When she got to the door, she whispered, 'Knock, knock.' There was no answer. Dawn was probably hunched inside, glaring at the door of her den as she stirred up some evil spell. Kirsty swallowed hard, then spoke louder. 'Dawn, Dawn, are you in?'

Kirsty could hear a weird snuffling from inside the room. She stepped closer to the door. Was the witch murmuring incantations? Was she mashing up toads or plucking the eyes from newts? Kirsty stood silent and still, just listening. What was that noise? Suddenly, she recognised it. It was crying. She put the tray down on the floor and tapped gently on the door.

'Dawn, can I come in?'

'No. What are you doing here? Go away.'

Kirsty tried the handle. The door opened. 'Dawn, what's the matter?' The room was gloomy; the lights hadn't been switched on yet. Kirsty could see a hump lying on the bed: Dawn.

The hump sniffled loudly. 'I said go away. What *are* you doing here anyway?'

'I came to ask you something. Are you all right?'

'You came to see if I was all right? Well, there's a first time for everything.'

'Why are you crying?' Kirsty stepped closer to the bed.

'Leave me alone.'

Kirsty was close enough now to see that Dawn was buried under her duvet. A stuffed teddy stuck his head out from under the covers – a stuffed teddy! Dawn had always laughed at Kirsty's battered old toy dog and here she was hiding in bed with her own teddy. Kirsty reached out to touch it, but as soon as her fingers came close the bear was whipped under the duvet with an angry growl.

'Go away!'

'Why are you crying? Did you get into trouble?' Kirsty peered cautiously at Dawn.

There was no answer.

'Did someone tell you off?' Kirsty asked.

Suddenly the duvet was thrown back and the glowering, evil witch raised herself up in her bed, eyes blazing and teeth bared. 'Will you just go away! I don't want to talk to you, or anyone. If you don't know why I'm upset, then I'm not going to tell you! Everything's all right for you, isn't it? Everything's easy! Well, that's not how it is for the rest of us. Go on, get out and leave me be!' The duvet was pulled back up and Dawn was hidden again.

Kirsty stepped back. She walked towards the door. She stopped and turned to the bed. 'Actually, everything is not all right for me. That's what I came here for. I was going to ask you to help. Ben said I should. I thought it was a stupid idea and I was right. You're too mean to help anyone.'

Kirsty pushed the tea and biscuits inside the door and then left.

Ben was sitting on the bottom step, waiting for Kirsty to come down. He stood when he saw her.

'We're on our own,' Kirsty said. 'Dawn's a mean, spiteful witch. She shouted at me for no reason. I couldn't even ask her about the allotment. She's upset, but she won't tell me why.'

'Yes, I heard her. I hoped she might have cheered up a bit.'

'You knew she was in that mood and you let me go

67

in anyway? I could have been turned into a frog! What's the matter with her?'

Ben shrugged. 'Dad, grandad. Stuff like that.'

'Oh.' Kirsty sighed. 'I'd better go home now. They'll be wondering where I am. Will you call me tomorrow? We can decide what to do next.'

'Sure. I might talk to Dawn again later,' Ben said.

Kirsty shrugged. 'I don't think Dawn will talk to you. But try if you want to.'

'You know, Kirsty, Dawn's not as tough as she makes out.'

'She should try being nicer to people,' snorted Kirsty.

Later that evening, Kirsty crouched down on the top stair, outside Dad's bedroom. Mum was downstairs, washing up after tea. Dad was in his room. He had eaten off a tray. Kirsty shuffled closer to the door, held her breath and listened. There was no sound coming from Dad's room. She laid her palm flat on the wood and stroked it softly. Dad hadn't come out of his room for days. She had carried the tray of food into his room earlier and he had hardly said a word to her. The room had been dark, with no lights on at all. He hadn't even said thank you when she put the tray down on his bedside table. He always said thank you! One time, he'd even said thank you to a cash machine! Kirsty let her hand rest on the door handle. Was Dad ever going to come out? Was he properly ill, like grandad had been?

Downstairs, the phone rang. It was probably someone calling to find out when Dad was coming to finish building their kitchen. Mum had spoken to a lot of them recently. Kirsty heard Mum answer it, but then she called upstairs, 'Kirsty, it's for you.' Kirsty turned away from the bedroom door and ran down.

'Kirsty?' It was Ben calling.

Kirsty cradled the phone against her ear. 'Hello. Is everything OK?'

'Listen – I can't talk long. I've done something stupid. I couldn't help it. I told my mum what's going on, and, anyway, she wants to help. Sorry. But, she says she can help. Can you come over after school tomorrow?'

'Yes, I suppose so. What's she going to do?'

'Dunno. Just come over and we'll find out.'

'OK,' Kirsty said. She gently dropped the receiver back into place. Mum was still in the kitchen, humming to herself. Kirsty smiled. Ben was on her side, whatever happened. And perhaps he'd let her play with his cool TV tomorrow.

WEDNESDAY

CHAPTER 10

'Juice?' Angela said. She put a glass of pink grapefruit crush down on a coaster in front of Kirsty. The juice was the same colour as Angela's painted fingernails.

'Thanks,' Kirsty whispered. She took a sip. It was so sharp it stung her mouth. Her eyes watered as she forced it down.

'Right.' Angela swished into one of the leather chairs that stood like sentries around the dining table. 'Ben has told me all about your little problem. Your dad putting his head in the sand again, is he?'

Kirsty frowned but didn't say anything. Ben looked down at his hands, clamped in his lap.

Angela smiled a TV presenter smile at them both. 'My dears, you should have come to me in the first place. Your father doesn't like to rock the boat. If you want to keep your grandad's allotment, you need someone effective on your side. Darlings, I've been getting my own way for years now. I'm a professional!' Angela laughed, a tinkly sound like a wind chime.

Ben seemed to curl deeper into his chair. Kirsty sat up straighter. This was really interesting – an adult on her side might be just what she needed! 'Do you really think you can help?' Kirsty asked.

Angela waved her arm in the air, as though she were bashing aside any problems. 'Of course I can help! As I understand it, the rotten council won't let you take the allotment on because you're too young. Is that it?'

Kirsty nodded her head slowly; that was mostly it.

'Well, dear, you need to start a campaign to force the council to change their mind, to bow to public pressure.'

'We held a demonstration,' Kirsty said, 'but it didn't work. We thought about a petition?'

'A petition? How ridiculous. No, dear, this isn't the nineties. Petitions run by some miserable old hag in the shopping centre don't cut it. What you need is a media campaign. You need to get headlines. "Council Caught in Kidz' Carrot Crisis", that sort of thing. We need to get some pictures of you looking all sad, with a trowel, some trees and whatnot in the background. You need to issue a press release, perhaps even start a website. Oh yes, you'll definitely need a website –

givemeagarden.com, kidzforfreedom.org, something like that –'

'Mum,' Ben interrupted. 'Mum, isn't that going a bit far?'

Angela stared at him, as though he had spoken in Latin. 'A bit far? Sweet pea, you can never go too far with a publicity campaign. Do you remember when I opened my first salon and I had that truck driving around town with that enormous wig on top of it? People were talking about it for weeks afterwards.'

'Yes,' Ben sighed. 'I know.'

'Or do you remember that time when I started doing glamorous nails and I had the local paper put fake fingernails in every copy to advertise it?'

Ben just nodded silently. The excitement that Kirsty had been feeling began to knot in her stomach. She remembered too well how upset Ben had been. Hundreds of people had called the paper to complain when loose fingernails dropped out of their morning paper and plopped into their cornflakes. Trails of broken nails followed paper boys down the streets. Newsagents had been finding fingernails on their floors for weeks afterwards. Ben had nearly died of shame.

'What we need is to think of a great stunt for you. Grab people's attention. A gimmick. How about a gardening marathon? Do you think you could dig for twenty-four hours?' Angela said.

A digging marathon? There was no way she could dig for that long! It would kill her! Kirsty bit her lip, then said, 'No, I don't think my mum would let me.'

'Hmm. Never mind, I'm sure we'll think of something,' Angela said. 'We can start with the photos. I'll call a photographer friend of mine. I can make you up to look a bit sad, you know – Oliver-Twist-meets-abandoned-puppy, that sort of thing. Wait here, I'll just go and make a phone call.'

Angela got up from her chair and swept out of the room with all her jewellery jangling.

'Wow,' Kirsty whispered.

'I know,' said Ben. 'I'm sorry.'

'What did she say she was going to do to me? Oliver Twist's puppy?'

'I have no idea. I should have just said no. I shouldn't have said anything to her in the first place. This is all my fault.'

Kirsty smiled at him. 'Yes. It probably is. But perhaps it will work? She seems to know what she's doing. I quite fancy the make-up bit anyway.'

'You would. I don't know. Perhaps she does want to help. But she might just want to get her salon in the newspapers. I bet she gets the photographs done with the shop in the background. I'm really sorry.' Ben's voice fell to a whisper.

'It can't be that bad,' Kirsty grinned.

A rustle of silk and the clanking of metal told them that Angela was back. She swung into the room, grinning like a cat in a cream factory. 'Well, dears, that's all sorted. Jermaine will meet us at the salon in twenty minutes. Chop-chop, we haven't got all day. Grab your coats. We've got a campaign to launch!'

CHAPTER 11

Inside the salon, Kirsty recognised the sharp tang
wafting from the dyes and bleaches, overlaid with the
heavy smell of lilies, which were dripping pollen on to
the purple reception desk. It was exciting. Ben, who
had seen the salon at least three thousand times more
than he wanted to, went straight to sit in a window
seat, with his back turned towards his mother. He took
out his mobile phone and jabbed at the buttons.

'OK, Kirsty, sweet pea.' Angela said. 'I'm going to do
your face a bit. Sit yourself down over there.' She
pointed to one of the purple salon chairs parked in
front of a full-length mirror. Kirsty hoisted herself up
into the seat. Her feet dangled miles from the floor,
even when she stretched out her toes. She could see
them in the mirror. Her dusty trainers looked funny
against the silver and purple of the salon.

is won't take long.'

sed her eyes as Angela whipped a sponge her face. It was covered in powder that went straight up her nose and into her throat. She struggled to hold in a sneeze-cough.

'This just takes away any nasty shine that would show up on camera. Keep your eyes closed. Good!' Angela said.

Kirsty felt a soft brush flick over her eyelids again and again.

'Open wide.'

Kirsty obligingly opened her mouth as though she were saying 'ah'. She heard Angela giggle. Wet, sloppy-feeling stuff was rubbed on to her lips.

'OK, open your eyes. This will give them sparkle.'

Kirsty lifted her lids to see a pipette like the ones they sometimes used in Science hovering in front of her eyes. Angela squeezed, and drops flew out of the pipette on to Kirsty's eyeball. She yelped.

'Don't worry, it's just eye drops. You look lovely.'

Kirsty's eyes slowly came back into focus as she blinked away the drops. She looked at herself in the mirror and gasped.

'Lovely, isn't it?' Angela said.

Kirsty's skin was pale. Her eyes peered out at her from the centre of gloomy black smears. Her lips had been painted ruby red. She felt a bit panicky all of a sudden. She looked like a panda who'd chewed a lipstick.

'Jermaine will be here soon. We'll get your story on the front page of the paper with you looking so touching!'

Kirsty slid out of her chair slowly. 'Is this how Oliver's puppy looked?' she said uncertainly.

Suddenly, the door to the salon sprang open. Dawn stepped in and looked around. Then she put her hands on her hips; her face was rigid with anger.

'Mum,' Dawn said. 'Why does Kirsty look like the bride of Dracula?'

Angela smiled warmly at her daughter. She spread her arms, waving Dawn into the salon. 'Sweetheart, how lovely. I wasn't expecting to see you here. Did I leave you a note? I don't remember.'

Dawn shook her head. 'No, you didn't. There was no sign of either of you when I got home. The house was empty, there was nothing for tea – then he texted.' Dawn jabbed her finger at Ben. 'He said I had to get down here quick to save Kirsty. Will someone please tell me what's going on?'

Kirsty's heart leapt in her chest. She blew a quick kiss in Ben's direction. Her lips left a greasy red smear on her fingers.

'What's wrong with Kirsty's face? She looks like she's been putting make-up on in the dark,' Dawn said.

'Don't be silly, darling. She looks perfect. Apart from that little smear there. Soon fix that.' Angela whipped a sponge over Kirsty's chin.

'Bit early for Halloween, isn't it?'

'Dawn!' Angela said sharply. 'You know how cruel the camera can be unless you're made up properly.'

Kirsty thought about the camera. Her stomach lurched in fear. She caught Dawn's eye and willed her to help. *Please, Dawn, please, Dawn*, she whispered silently, over and over again.

'What camera?' Dawn asked. Her voice was as cold and hard as the chrome chandeliers that hung from the salon ceiling.

'Kirsty's going to be in the paper,' Angela said.

'Mum. One last time, what is going on?'

'Oh dear, you sound so serious. All that's happening is that I am helping little Kirsty get a bit of publicity, bring her plight to the world, that sort of thing.'

'What plight?'

'Well, to keep your grandad's allotment, of course. We're starting the campaign right here, right now. Well, in about ten minutes, I should think. Jermaine is usually a little bit late.'

Kirsty looked at Dawn. Dawn looked back. Kirsty

couldn't tell what she was thinking. Would she help? Or would she just laugh? Kirsty bit her lip; she could taste the greasy lipstick on her teeth.

Dawn seemed to make up her mind. 'Kirsty,' she said. 'Get that stuff off your face. Ben, get your coat. Mum, get a grip.'

Kirsty leaped up from the chair and ran to the sink. She turned on the shower attachment and soaked the front of her jumper, but managed to get most of the make-up off.

'But what –' Angela stuttered. 'Dawnie, what's the matter?'

'Mum,' Dawn said. 'I'm sure that Kirsty appreciates your help. Oh wait, no, actually, I don't suppose she does. So stop helping.'

Kirsty came away from the sink dripping water and slimy gunk. She turned to Angela. 'Mrs Jenkins, thank you very much for your help, but Dawn's right. This is something I need to do by myself.'

Ben came and stood next to her. 'No,' he said. 'Not by yourself. Me and Dawn will help.'

Kirsty grinned. 'Brilliant!'

CHAPTER 12

Outside the salon, Dawn marched off ahead. Kirsty ran to catch up. Ben struggled behind, trying to force his arms into his coat and walk at the same time.

'Dawn!' Kirsty shouted.

Dawn swung away from the road, heading towards the park. Kirsty moved faster. Why was Dawn running away? Had she changed her mind already? What was going on?

'What's going on?' Kirsty yelled as loudly as she could. Dawn stopped. She turned slowly. Kirsty recognised the look on Dawn's face; if there had been a jumper handy, or a shoe, or a book, Dawn would be throwing it at her right now. What had happened to the Dawn who charged into the salon like a knight on horseback? Kirsty walked towards her warily.

'Dawn, are you OK?' Kirsty whispered.

85

'Yes. No.' Dawn looked angry. 'I don't know why you want the allotment anyway. It was Grandad who knew about gardens, not you. You just used to play there. The only thing you've ever grown by yourself was cress on cotton wool in playgroup. And that went mouldy.'

Beside the pavement, there was a low wall, marking the edge of someone's garden. Dawn sat down heavily on it. Kirsty stood in front of her, trying to read her face. She looked tired and cross, but she also looked sad. Kirsty leaned in closer. Dawn covered her face with her hands. Then Kirsty's hand did something strange, as if it had taken on a life of its own. It stretched outwards and settled on the back of Dawn's head, stroking her hair. Kirsty held her breath. What would Dawn do? Move away? Shrug her off? Bite her hand? Dawn didn't move at all. They stayed like that, close together, Kirsty's fingers resting on Dawn's soft hair. Then Ben finally caught up with them.

'Wow,' he said. 'Is this an Oprah moment?'

'Shove off,' Dawn muttered into her hands, but Kirsty could tell that she was smiling. She lifted her hand away as Dawn looked up.

'Are you missing Grandad?' Kirsty whispered gently. Dawn seemed to stiffen again, as though she were growing prickles. 'Cos I am,' Kirsty said. 'And I miss

Dad too. And I'm worried that we'll never get him back.'

Dawn's prickles disappeared. Her eyes looked strangely watery. 'Yes,' she sniffed. 'Me too.'

'Totally Oprah,' Ben muttered.

'Shove off,' Kirsty said.

Dawn laughed properly. Ben scowled for a second, then started chuckling himself.

'Will you help us, then?' Kirsty asked quietly.

'Oh, I suppose so. As long as none of my friends find out. If anyone sees me, I'll have to pretend I don't know you. What do you want me to do?'

'Come to the allotment tomorrow. It's too late to go now – Mum'll be wondering where I am. But come tomorrow, after school, and we'll all decide on what we're going to do next.'

THURSDAY

CHAPTER 13

At the allotment, Kirsty sat on an old sack in front of the shed and told Dawn the whole problem. Ben listened too. 'Grandad asked me to look after the allotment for him, so I promised I would. But then I came here and Mr Thomas from the council said I couldn't. I was too young and I wasn't on the waiting list. Mum agrees with him. I don't know what Dad thinks, cos he hasn't been around to ask. Mr Thomas said on Monday that it takes two weeks to find new owners. That means we've only got a week left to change everyone's minds.'

'What have you done so far?' Dawn asked.

'I spoke to Mr Thomas, but it didn't go very well. I followed him into the museum, see, and I don't think he liked that. So that didn't work. And then we did a demonstration, but the fire brigade came.'

'What?' Dawn yelped.

'It's OK. The police haven't come after us,' Kirsty said.

'What!'

'Nothing,' Ben said quickly. 'Then there was Mum's media campaign that you got us out of.'

Dawn shook her head. 'So you whined at the man from the council, you bothered the emergency services and then you didn't get in the paper. Not much of a campaign, is it?'

Kirsty shuffled uncomfortably on the sack. Why was Dawn always so irritating? 'Well, what would you have done?'

'Oh, I don't know. You've started right, I guess. You just have to think a bit bigger now.'

'That's just what Mum said about the media campaign,' Ben mumbled.

'I'm not talking bigger like that. I meant more sophisticated, more devious.'

'What kind of devious?' Kirsty grinned; it sounded like Dawn had an idea!

'It's time to start getting creative.' Dawn said firmly. 'This allotment is going to the next person on the waiting list, isn't it? Well then, it's easy. All we have to do is make you the next person on the list.'

'But how can we do that?' Ben asked.

'What am I, Cunning Plans R Us? I said I'd help, not do everything. You two need to think here too.'

They sat in silence for a while. The cold was beginning to spread through Kirsty, even though she was wrapped up from head to toe. Her nose felt wet, like a Labrador's; any minute it would start to drip into her lap. She rubbed her nose on her sleeve and thought about what Dawn had said.

'The waiting list would be in Mr Thomas's office, wouldn't it? On his computer?' Kirsty asked.

'Yes,' Ben said. 'He wouldn't take any work home with him, I don't think. He likes to forget about his job as soon as he leaves his office.'

'So,' Kirsty grinned. 'All we need to do is get into his office and change the name at the top of the list.'

'How can we get in without him seeing us?'

'Don't worry about that,' Dawn smiled. 'There's always a way.'

'Wait though.' Kirsty stopped grinning. 'We can't put my name at the top of the list – he'll recognise it. And he'll recognise me when he comes to tell me that I've got an allotment.'

Ben shook his head. 'There is no way that Mr Thomas tells people in person when he gives them an allotment. He wouldn't make a big fuss. He just sends them a letter, I bet. So all we need to do is change your name a bit and he'll send you a letter.'

'What if he's already sent a letter to the new owners?' Dawn asked.

Kirsty shook her head. 'No, he hasn't. He told me at the museum that he was going to write his report this week and get new tenants next week.'

'So we still have time!' Ben said. 'It's brilliant. So simple, so . . . devious.' He smiled at Dawn.

Kirsty felt her heart swell with excitement. It was a great idea, but would it work? 'How can we get into his office when he isn't there?' she asked.

Dawn grinned. 'I go and see him, and cause a diversion. You change the list. Easy. Like stealing sweets from a baby.'

'Stealing sweets from a baby is hard,' Ben said. 'They cry and throw tantrums.'

'Shut up,' Dawn said. 'It's easy. I'll make an appointment.' She pulled out her mobile phone. She sounded confident, but Kirsty noticed that her hands were shaking; she had to dial directory enquiries twice before she got the number right.

Kirsty and Ben stayed absolutely quiet while Dawn called the council.

'Hello, er, Mr Thomas? Hi. I'm Dawn, er, Jennings. I'm calling because I'm doing a project at school. On, er, green cities. I was hoping I could come and interview you. It would really help. Please, just five minutes.' There was a long pause. 'That would be perfect!' Dawn said. 'Thank you.' She hung up the phone.

'Well?' Ben asked.

'I'm meeting him tomorrow after school. In his office at 3.40.'

Kirsty shivered with excitement. They were getting close.

CHAPTER 14

Kirsty said goodbye to Ben and Dawn and cycled home. She let herself into the house. She stood in the hall and let the door close gently behind her. The soft click of the latch was the only sound she could hear. It was strange – way too quiet. Before, when Dad was well, this would have been the noisiest time of day – everyone coming home and shouting hellos, telling stories about their day, and Dad, right in the middle of it all, laughing. Instead, it was just silent.

'Hello?' she said softly. Were Mum and Dad even in?

She heard a sound from upstairs. Burglars? Was she alone in the house with burglars? Her heartbeat speeded up as she crept to the bottom of the staircase.

'Shh!' It was Mum, hissing down from the landing. 'Your dad's sleeping.'

Kirsty felt her fear turn into something else. Anger.

Dad was always sleeping! Why wouldn't he get up? What was going on? And all Mum would say was 'shh'. She was like a broken record. Well, Kirsty wasn't going to shush.

She stomped into the front room. Her DVDs were arranged on the bottom shelf. There were lots of them, but her collection was nothing compared to Dad's records. He had hundreds and hundreds of them stacked along the top shelves. The records hadn't been touched in a long time though. Before he got so tired, Dad liked to rearrange his collection. He'd change it every week, sometimes putting it in alphabetical order, sometimes in date order, sometimes even according to the colour of the cover, so that the records looked like a rainbow stretching along the wall. Kirsty liked to copy him. Just now, both collections were arranged in order of favourites. Her favourite film, *The Wizard of Oz*, was first and Dad's favourite album was first in his collection.

Kirsty took the record down from the shelf. There was dust on the cover. Each letter in the band's name, Sex Pistols, was written in a different size, as though each letter had been torn from a newspaper. There had been a row once about that album. It had a rude title and Mum had said that Dad shouldn't let Kirsty see it. Dad had said that Kirsty was his daughter too and she should know about the things he cared about. Dad had won.

No one had played it for a long time. Kirsty looked up at the ceiling. Dad's bed was directly above her. Kirsty slid the record from its sleeve. It was sleek and black, the music printed on it in bumps and grooves that you could touch. She held it by the rim and looked at it. Dad knew all the lyrics to each song. He used to yell them as loud as he could, not caring that the neighbours would bang on the wall. He used to jump up and down to the music, not dancing, just throwing himself about like a mad thing.

Kirsty lifted the glass lid of the record player, then moved the stylus gently. The speakers hissed and crackled for a minute, then roared into life with the first tune. Drums thumped, a wild guitar joined in and then the singer, shouting each line until his voice seemed to be breaking. The speakers shuddered with the noise. Kirsty put down the sleeve and started dancing the way that Dad did, bounding into the air, shaking her hands and head, slamming back down to the floor. The whole room juddered with movement and music. Could Dad hear this? She didn't know the words like Dad did, but she started yelling the ones she knew anyway. Was he listening? Would he come down and join in?

'Kirsty!' The door opened. Kirsty stopped dancing. Mum crossed the room and lifted the stylus off the record. The silence was shocking.

'What are you doing?' Mum hissed.

'I was just listening to music.'

'On full volume? When your dad's trying to rest upstairs?'

Kirsty didn't answer.

Mum frowned. 'What were you thinking?'

'I thought, I thought Dad might like it. He hasn't listened to it in ages.' Kirsty hung her head.

Mum sighed. A moment passed. Mum sat down on the sofa and patted the seat beside her. She wanted Kirsty to sit. So Kirsty sat. 'Kirsty, it's hard for your dad just now. You know that, don't you? Your grandad was *his* dad.'

'I know. But he's been in his room for ever.'

Mum smiled, but it was a sad smile. 'It does feel a bit like that, doesn't it? But we have to give him time.'

'How *much* time?'

'Oh, Kirsty. You just have to be patient. I'm sure he'll be right as rain soon. He just needs some peace and quiet. Give him space, OK?'

Kirsty nodded slowly. She stood up and lifted the record off the deck. She slipped it back in its cover. 'Can I at least dust them?' she asked.

Mum nodded. 'OK. Dad would like that. I'll get you a cloth.'

Kirsty put the album back on the shelf, in first place. In the horrible quiet, it felt as though she was hiding it away.

FRIDAY

CHAPTER 15

At 3.35 p.m. exactly, Kirsty met Dawn and Ben at the council building. Kirsty, taking no chances, had wrapped her head round and round with the longest scarf she could find. She could hardly see out of it.

'Why are you dressed like an Egyptian mummy?' Dawn asked.

'It's complicated. Well, not complicated, exactly –'

'If they recognise us, we're in trouble. The fire alarm, see,' Ben butted in, pulling his own hood down over his forehead.

Dawn rolled her eyes. 'You two are impossible,' she said and led the way inside.

Kirsty kept her head down and let Dawn do the talking.

'Help you?' the man at the reception desk said, without looking up.

'I've got an appointment with Mr Thomas,' Dawn said.

'Mr Thomas gardens or Mr Thomas school dinners?'

'Er . . . Mr Thomas gardens,' said Dawn, thinking quickly.

'Lift. Third floor. Three doors down.'

Inside the lift, Kirsty pushed the button marked '3'. She knew she was too old to be bothered about pushing the buttons in lifts, but somehow today she felt quite young. It was something to do with the queasy feeling in her stomach. *My first proper crime*, she thought; setting off the alarm had just been an accident.

'We'll not get caught, will we?' Kirsty asked.

Dawn shrugged. 'Well, if we do, you're too young to go to prison. Me and Ben might have to face justice, I suppose.'

'Really?' Ben's voice sounded squeaky.

'No, dummy. All we're doing is adding a made-up name to a list. We're not stealing the *Mona Lisa*.'

'Then why am I so frightened?' Ben whispered.

Dawn snorted. 'You're always frightened.'

The lift doors opened. The corridor stretched out for miles in front of them. The square ceiling tiles and the square carpet tiles seemed to come together at some far point in the distance. Kirsty thought it was like looking down a well.

Dawn went ahead, walking with her head up and her back straight. She looked so brave, Kirsty felt better just being with her. They could hear the muffled sounds of phone calls and typing coming from behind most of the doors. Nameplates told them who was working behind each one. The third door on the right had a small metal plaque with 'Mr Thomas' engraved on it. Below, someone had added a Post-it note with 'gardens' written on it.

'There's nowhere to hide,' Kirsty whispered.

'I can see that,' Dawn said.

'We have to hide.'

'Thanks again for stating the obvious.'

'Dawn, don't be mean.' Ben said.

'Sorry.'

Ben moved past Mr Thomas's office to the next door. There was no nameplate on it, just a lighter patch of wood where a plaque had been. He pressed his ear to the door and stood still. Then he turned back and waved. 'In here.'

Ben tried the handle and the door swung open. The room was empty. The light was dim. Kirsty and Dawn followed Ben inside.

'This is good,' Dawn whispered. 'You'll hear when

you can come in and get to the computer.'

'How will we know?' Kirsty said.

'Don't worry. I've got a plan. You'll know.'

Dawn slipped out and closed the door behind her. Ben and Kirsty crouched down to wait.

The office was small. There was just enough room for a desk and a chair and Kirsty and Ben. The wall which divided it from Mr Thomas's office had a map of the city on it, dotted with drawing-pins, as though it had measles. The walls were thin enough for them to hear Dawn knock on Mr Thomas's door. They heard his gruff reply. It was difficult to make out what was being said – it was too muffled – but they could hear the rumble of the conversation through the walls.

'What if she can't get him to leave?' Ben whispered.

'She will. Just wait.'

They sat crouched up against the wall for what seemed like an age. They could hear a kettle boil and the sound of Mr Thomas stirring a drink. He gave short answers to Dawn's questions. The moments passed.

'She's not going to do it,' Ben said.

'Shh.'

Suddenly a shriek sliced the air. They heard a chair fall and then a frightened whimper.

'It's Dawn,' Ben gasped. 'She's hurt.'

'Did he hurt her? Does he know?'

'Dunno.'

Mr Thomas's door opened; they could hear him clearly now. 'Come on, we'll get cold water on that. There's a first-aid station, a first aider. This way.' Then the sound of Dawn sobbing moving off down the corridor.

'He's out of the office!' Kirsty grinned. 'Come on. Now!'

The coast was clear. They slipped into Mr Thomas's empty office. Ben rushed straight to his desk. His PC glowed blue.

'Look at that,' Kirsty said. She was pointing at a postcard that was Blu-tacked to the monitor – it was a picture of the city museum from the street. 'He must really love it there.'

'There's no time for nosing about,' Ben said. He took the mouse and started clicking open folders. He was breathing fast. *Click*, *click*, *click*. 'I can't find it!' he said. 'It's not here!'

'Look harder. Quick. He'll be back any second.' Kirsty ran back to the door and strained hard to hear any noise in the corridor outside.

Ben's hand flicked rapidly from side to side, opening windows, following leads through folders and files, his eyebrows drawn together in concentration.

'Here!' he said. 'I've got it! I just need to add a new

line for you. Well, for Katy Jennings, actually.'

Footsteps approached. Kirsty held in a squeak, feeling prickles of fear spreading all over. She eased open the door, just far enough to see. Mr Thomas was walking back towards his office. Dawn followed behind him, clutching her arm.

'Oh no,' Kirsty said. 'Ben, you better have finished. He's back!'

'Two seconds.'

'We haven't got two seconds!'

Kirsty dropped down low and peered around the door; she didn't dare stick her head out too far. He was ten metres away, eight metres, six metres. He was going to catch them! Dawn struggled to see past Mr Thomas's bulk. She moved left and right, trying to see the office door. Then she saw Kirsty peeping out at her. Dawn's eyebrows shot up and her eyes saucered wide. She hurled herself to the floor, landing heavy and hard. Mr Thomas whipped around at the noise. He had his back to the office door!

'Ben! Now!' Kirsty hissed.

'Done!'

'Move. The lift!' Kirsty said. Kirsty pulled the door open just enough for the two of them to slip out of the office and pelt down to the lift. Dawn groaned louder and doubled up in pain. Ben bashed the call button again and again. Mr Thomas was bound to turn any second and they were right in view.

'Stairs!' Kirsty whispered and ploughed through the doorway just next to the lift. They were in a stairwell; grey steps led down to the floor below. Kirsty leaned against the door, holding it closed. She fought down the giggles. She could still hear Dawn moaning in the corridor behind her, and Mr Thomas starting to panic.

'Do you need a doctor? An ambulance? Are you hurt?'

Abruptly the moaning stopped. 'Oh no, I'm fine. Just fell over. I can't believe what a klutz I'm being today. Thanks very much for meeting me. Bye!'

Kirsty stepped away from the door just as Dawn burst through. Her face was red and blotchy – had she been crying? No, Kirsty realised. She was laughing – killing herself laughing, but straining to be quiet.

'We'd best get out of here,' Kirsty whispered. 'Before Dawn has a heart attack.'

'Are you OK? Did you burn yourself?' Ben sounded anxious.

Dawn rolled her eyes. 'Of course not. I'm not an idiot. I was pretending, you doofus. Though I think I bruised my bum when I threw myself on the floor.'

Kirsty grinned at Dawn. 'You're brilliant,' she said. 'And I'm top of the list!'

SATURDAY

CHAPTER 16

The next day, Dawn and Ben stayed over, as usual. But, for Kirsty, nothing felt quite normal. On Saturday morning she sat in the passenger seat of the race car. Ben was driving. He revved the engine quietly. They didn't speak. Then Kirsty's door opened.

'Can I get in?' Dawn asked.

Ben swivelled in his seat. Kirsty raised her eyebrows. Dawn never, ever, ever, came to play in the car. But today she was wrapped up in a duffle coat and a scarf, as if she was planning on being outside for a while. With them.

'OK,' Kirsty said. 'But you have to sit in the back.'

Dawn rolled her eyes, then slammed the door. It looked as though she was going to storm back into the house. Kirsty felt a stab of disappointment. Odd.

But then the back door opened and Dawn threw

herself on to the seat. 'Where are we going?' she asked.

Ben looked around warily. 'Are you sure you want to come?'

'Course.'

'Where do you want to go?'

Dawn thought for a minute. 'Somewhere warm. I'm freezing. How about Florida?'

'But it's a car. You can't *drive* to Florida. It's over the sea.'

'Well,' Dawn said slowly. 'Now it's a plane.'

'Oh, OK.' Ben eased the car into gear and then revved the jet engines loudly. 'Engaging thruster engines. Deploying wings. Doors to automatic. Ready for take-off.' He flicked the switches around the steering wheel. Then, with a full-throated roar, the g-force threw everyone back into their seats.

Kirsty felt the weight of their acceleration hit them like an elephant charging. At this speed they would reach America in minutes! The waves of the Atlantic Ocean rose and fell below them. They flew through a dark bank of clouds and turbulence juddered the plane sickeningly. Then, they were through the storm and sunlight danced over the water. Kirsty looked down. 'I can see the Statue of Liberty!' She pointed at Mum's bird table.

'Turn left then. Florida isn't far,' Dawn said. Ben

pulled down hard on the wheel and they all leaned into the turn.

'There's Disneyland. And the Everglades,' Ben pointed. 'We're coming in to land. Brace yourselves.'

Kirsty rammed her feet up against the dashboard as the car began its descent. They hit the runway hard, then bounced back into the air. Everyone lifted out of their seats. Kirsty's stomach rose and fell, shifting her breakfast unpleasantly. With a final thud, they were on US soil.

'Sorry about the landing,' Ben said. 'The heat made the wheels expand. We're lucky we didn't have to crash-land.'

'It's all right,' Dawn said. 'It's amazing that we got here in a Ford Escort at all.'

Kirsty smiled. She couldn't remember Dawn being this nice ever – at least not for years. She turned to face the back seat. 'Florida was a good choice.'

'Yeah, well. Anywhere's better than here.'

There was a sudden silence in the car. Kirsty sat back down in her seat and stared out of the window; condensation had formed on the glass and drops of water had rolled down and made small puddles on the black rubber.

'I'm sorry,' Dawn said. 'I didn't mean here with you. I meant here in general. With Dad.'

Kirsty put her finger up to the glass and dragged it downwards. It left a thick snake-trail behind.

'Don't you think it's weird how Dad never leaves his room?' Dawn asked.

'Yes,' Kirsty said quietly.

'Has your mum said anything about it? Why he won't get out of bed?'

Kirsty thought about what Mum had said last week. 'She says he just needs time. And peace and quiet.'

Dawn made a snorting noise in the back seat. 'He's had loads of peace and quiet. That's why we're all outside in a broken-down car in the freezing cold. I'm sick of it.'

'My mum says he'll be fine. We just have to leave him be for a while.'

'Yes. But do you think she's right though?' Dawn sounded impatient.

Kirsty didn't answer straight away. Was Mum right? Would Dad get better by himself? Kirsty remembered how Dad had looked when he came out of Grandad's room at the hospital. Mum had half-carried Dad into the corridor. He had leaned against her as though his legs weren't strong enough to hold him, his face white, his hands shaking. It had been like seeing Dad's ghost – as though he had been the one who died, not Grandad. Would rest be enough to make him better?

'I don't know,' Kirsty said finally. 'He's very sad, I think. I'd be sad if Dad died. It's too horrible even to think about.'

''Course you'd be sad. We all would. But would you lock yourself in your room for two weeks?'

'It hasn't been two weeks. Not quite.'

Dawn leaned forwards between the front seats so that she was right up close to Ben and Kirsty. 'It's been too long. I think something needs to be done.'

'What sort of thing?' Ben asked.

Dawn sighed. 'That's the trouble. I don't know.'

MONDAY

CHAPTER 17

Kirsty woke early, before her alarm. Would the letter come today? Was the allotment going to be hers? She crept quietly out of bed, so as not to wake Dawn. She pulled on her coat and waited outside the front door for the postman with a tingly feeling running through her body. It was like waiting for presents on Christmas Eve – unbearable and brilliant at the same time.

'Morning,' Kirsty said to the postman.

'Glorious day,' he said.

Kirsty looked up at the low grey sky. You probably had to be a cheerful sort of person to be a postman. She smiled. 'Any post for Katy Jennings?'

'Sadly no. However, I do have a hundredweight of supermarket flyers. Perhaps I could interest you in taking a few handfuls of those?'

'No thanks. See you tomorrow.'

TUESDAY

CHAPTER 18

Still no letter.

WEDNESDAY

CHAPTER 19

Nothing. Nil. Nought. Nowt. Zip. Zero.

Sweet dang doodle diddly-squat.

THURSDAY

CHAPTER 20

Kirsty dragged her school bag behind her on the way home. It banged against her ankles, but she didn't bother lifting it higher. There had been no letter that morning either. Had it gone wrong? Had Mr Thomas found out? Were the police on their trail for breaking into the office?

Kirsty opened the front door and dropped her bag down on the mat.

'Kirsty?'

'Hi, Mum.'

'Come here, please.'

Kirsty shuffled into the living room. Mum was sitting on the couch. She had an envelope in one hand and a letter in the other. Kirsty could just make out the red crest of the council at the top of the paper. Oh no. This was bad.

'A really strange letter came in the second post this afternoon. A *really* strange letter.'

The second post! She'd forgotten all about that! This was a disaster.

Mum shook the letter. 'It's not for us. It's for someone called Katy Jennings. And they've given her an allotment. On Grandad's old site. Have you got any idea why they would have sent us this?'

How on earth could Kirsty explain that one? Was there a convincing story just waiting to be thought of? Was there a brilliant excuse she could use? Kirsty sped through some of her favourite excuses. *I was abducted by aliens so I couldn't do my homework. I didn't make the mess – a runaway train raced through and sent everything flying. I can't wash up just now – a troupe of dancing elephants need their tutus altered before tonight's big show.* They were all great excuses, but none of them would get her out of this trouble. There must be something she could tell Mum.

'Kirsty, did you hear what I said?'

None of those excuses were any good. It had to be something believable. Something simple. Kirsty took a deep breath. 'The council must have got confused and made a mistake. They must have got the addresses muddled. But it's a good mistake, isn't it? They've given it to us, just like Grandad wanted. It's like fate or something.'

Mum looked doubtful. 'Don't you think it's weird that they got our address? Seems a bit fishy.'

'No, no. Not at all. It must have been on Grandad's file, you know. And the computer just got confused. Computers go wrong all the time. Remember when Ben almost bought a house on the internet by mistake?'

'Of course I remember. I nearly had a heart attack.'

'Well, this will just be like that – the computer doing something weird. But, if I keep the allotment, I can keep my promise to Grandad too. I can keep it now, can't I?'

Mum stared hard at the letter. She didn't speak. She stroked the edge of the paper with her thumb. Kirsty focused hard on Mum's face, trying to send hypnotic signals into her brain. *Please say yes, please say yes, please say yes.*

'I'm sorry Kirsty, but I can't just say yes. The whole thing seems odd. I'm going to have to speak to the council about it. Whoever this Katy Jennings is, she's been waiting for this letter. It isn't fair that we take it from her.'

'But, Mum. What about fate? What about destiny?' Kirsty was getting desperate.

'We'll see. I'll speak to the council and see what they

say. I can't say fairer than that.'

This was worse than a disaster. The most terrible thing that could happen was for Mum to speak to Mr Thomas. It would all come out: how they'd followed him, the fire alarm, perhaps even the break-in if they investigated hard enough. Mum couldn't call the council.

'Don't speak to the council, please. If we don't tell them, they won't find out. Please, Mum?'

'Kirsty, stop it. You can't just keep it. There's too much going on right now, with your dad and every-thing. We talked about this. I know you miss Grandad, we all do, but you have to let this go.'

'What? Like Dad's doing? He's not letting it go, hiding away in bed all the time, is he?'

As soon as the words were out of her mouth, Kirsty wished that she could claw them back in again. Mum looked shocked. The room suddenly felt very small, as though the walls had rushed in around them.

'Kirsty Anne Jenkins,' Mum said slowly. 'That's a horrible thing to say.'

Kirsty felt her face flush. She really hadn't meant to say anything. But she had. She took a deep breath.

'Mum,' she said quietly. 'What's wrong with Dad?'

It was as though a shutter had clanged closed. Mum's face was blank. 'There's nothing wrong with your father. Now go and get changed out of your school uniform.'

'But, Mum –'

'I *said* go and get changed, Kirsty.'

Kirsty turned towards the stairs. There was no point arguing.

CHAPTER 21

Kirsty wiped her eyes and threw the tissue on to her bedroom floor. She wasn't going to cry! No way! This wasn't over yet. She was going to keep her promise to Grandad. She was so close! The allotment was so nearly hers. Well, it was Katy Jennings' and that was close enough. She wasn't going to give up yet. If Mum called Mr Thomas tomorrow then it would all be over. She had to stop Mum from calling the council. That would buy some time at least until the weekend when Ben and Dawn would be around to help.

Could she cut the phone wires? She wasn't exactly sure what that meant, but it was what murderers did in the movies to stop their victims calling the police. Kirsty imagined herself dressed in black, climbing up the telegraph pole, a pair of pliers in one hand and an evil laugh in her throat. No, it was no good. She wouldn't know which wires to cut. She'd probably electrocute herself.

But what about the phone itself though? Could she break that? Hitting it with a hammer would probably do the trick. Mum might guess it was her though. She shouldn't smash it up; she should disable it. That was the word. As soon as Mum was in bed, the phone was history. Kirsty smiled again, the tears all gone.

'I'm just calling you so I can look at the phone,' Kirsty said.

'What?' Ben answered.

'I just need to look at it. What do you think the screw does on the bit you hold?'

'I dunno. What are you going on about?'

'I bet it's important. They don't put screws in if they're not important do they?'

'Kirsty. This is the weirdest phone call I've ever had.'

'Good. I'll see you tomorrow. We have to talk.' Kirsty hung up

It was easy to stay awake that night. It was easy to wait for proper, silent and still darkness. At midnight, Kirsty got out of bed slowly, so it wouldn't creak. She reached

for the screwdriver she had hidden under the bed. Got it. She crept out of the room into the dark hall. The James Bond music started in her head – dum di-di dum, dum; dum, di-di dum, dum. She pressed her back to the wall, listening for other secret agents. There was silence, but there was no knowing how many booby traps were laid for her. Each step was careful and precise. She was grateful now for the special stealth catsuit M had given her back at the lab; she would only show up as a strange bit of distortion on the security feeds. Good job too that the screwdriver could shoot tranquiliser darts.

Down the stairs, into the hall. Still total silence. A sliver of light came in through the window in the front door. This was too easy. There should at least have been guard dogs. She reached the phone and lifted the receiver. The burr of the dial tone sounded loud in the hallway. Her heart rate picked up. Enemy forces might be alerted any second. She worked quickly. Soon the screw was out and the phone fell open in her hands. Inside the receiver there was a jumble of wires and two small disks about the size of a fifty pence piece. They looked important. Kirsty was sure the phone wouldn't work without them. It took just a few seconds for her to pop out the connecting wire and the disks came free. She fitted the phone back together and tightened the screw. Mission accomplished.

She was back in her room in an instant – no alarms sounded, no warning shots were fired. And the phone was out of commission.

FRIDAY

CHAPTER 22

After school, Kirsty came home to find Mum in the front garden. She was wrapped up in Dad's big winter coat, watching the birds.

'Hi, Mum.'

'Hello, love. Nice day?' Mum sounded distracted, as though she wasn't thinking about Kirsty at all.

'I suppose. You?'

'I suppose. The phone's broken. I asked your dad to mend it, but . . .' She pulled the edges of the coat tighter around herself. 'At least Dad's customers can't get through. Honestly, some of them, it's like kitchen cabinets are a matter of life or death.'

'Mum,' Kirsty said slowly. 'Is everything OK?'

Kirsty looked at Mum square on, their eyes locking for a second. Kirsty wasn't sure what she saw in Mum's eyes. Sadness, worry, anger? It was like a mix of all of them. Then it was gone.

'Of course it is, love. I think I'll have to get an engineer for that dratted phone.' Mum looked at the birds again. 'They'll be making their nests before long,' she said. 'Go on indoors. Your brother and sister will be here soon.'

'Half—,' Kirsty stopped. She was going to say half-sister, but she didn't quite want to. She smiled a little at herself, then went inside.

Ben and Dawn arrived just before tea. There was no time to talk. Kirsty was desperate to tell them just what had been happening, but Mum was there all the time. Kirsty forced down her baked potato as fast as she could. When the meal was over she grabbed Ben's arm and pulled him out of his chair. 'We'll wash up,' Kirsty said. 'And Dawn can dry. Why don't you go and put your feet up, Mum?'

'Washing up without being asked! Who are you and what have you done with my daughter?'

'Very funny, Mum.' Kirsty shoved some plates into Ben's hands and steered him into the kitchen. Moments later Dawn arrived, carrying the salt and pepper.

'From your crazy behaviour I guess we have a

problem?' Dawn asked.

Kirsty turned the taps on full. The pipes clanged and banged noisily. She looked back into the living room. Mum had switched on the telly.

'Shh,' Kirsty whispered. 'Yes, we have a problem. Mum's going to ring the council and tell them they made a mistake. I broke the phone, but she'll get it fixed. I reckon on Monday the whole thing is going to blow.'

'What do you mean "blow"?' Ben asked, splashing plates into the water. Dawn banged an oven tray loudly.

'I mean, *KABOOM*. Explosion, mushroom cloud. I mean the council and Mum will find out what we did and the whole thing will blow up. We'll be grounded. For ever.'

Ben nodded slowly. 'I see. You're right. *Kaboom*. What are we going to do?'

'Think,' Kirsty said with determination. 'We think all night if we have to.'

Kirsty thought all evening. But nothing came to her. Every time she tried to imagine a way out of this mess, she found herself thinking about Dad. Grandad was already gone, his allotment was going and it felt like

Dad had left too. But he was just in his room! As she cleaned her teeth before bedtime, she thought about it some more. How could someone be there but at the same time it feel as though they were a million miles away?

It made her cross.

She spat the toothpaste into the sink and rinsed the brush.

It wasn't fair of him to be like this.

She put the brush back in its holder.

He shouldn't be like this. He was her *dad*.

Kirsty opened the bathroom door, but instead of turning left to go to her room, she turned right. Towards Dad's room. She could hear the sound of the TV on downstairs; Mum and Dawn and Ben were watching something noisy. Mum wouldn't hear her going into Dad's room.

'Dad?' she said.

The room was dark and smelled funny, like the air had been breathed too often. Dad was just a shape in the gloom. He shouldn't be in here like this – it was all wrong!

'Dad?' Kirsty walked closer to the bed.

The shape under the duvet shifted, turning over to face her. 'Kirsty? Is that you?' Dad's voice was hardly more than a croak.

Suddenly her anger evaporated, as though it had never even been. She felt her eyes sting with tears. It was like visiting Grandad all over again. Kirsty wanted to rush over and crawl in next to him, to give him a tight hug, the kind he used to give her when she was upset.

But she couldn't.

He still felt too far away, even though she was in the same room as him.

'Kirsty, what do you want?' Dad's voice was flat and dull.

'I wanted to say goodnight.'

'Goodnight,' he said.

'Are you getting up tomorrow?' Kirsty asked quietly.

Dad didn't speak; the sound of the TV coming from downstairs seemed loud in Kirsty's ears. Then Dad said, 'Go to bed, Kirsty.'

Kirsty backed away. It was as though Dad was turning into a stranger.

SATURDAY

CHAPTER 23

Kirsty watched the sunrise with bleary eyes. For a moment, its bright rays glancing in through a gap in her curtains seemed cheerful. It was nearly spring. But then she remembered there was a row coming, like dark clouds in the distance. She got up, shivering as she pulled on her dressing gown. Downstairs, she made herself a bowl of cereal and sat down on the kitchen step to eat it.

The house was quiet, except for the crunch of the cereal in her mouth. She could hear early traffic pass by in front of the house and, after a while, the gurgling in the pipes that meant the heating was switching itself on. She shovelled another spoonful into her mouth, splashing milk down her chin. It seemed easier to think when the house was so still . . . like a monastery in a kung-fu film. She was a monk in a mountain fortress. Eagles soared above and the whole misty valley opened before her. She was seeking wisdom, and deadly fighting skills. She put down the bowl and pulled her legs into the lotus position, each ankle tucked under the opposite knee. She took a breath of cold, fresh air and focused her mind.

There were two problems, both part of a bigger picture. First, Dad. Last night, in his room, Kirsty had realised that he was moving further and further away. Time and space just weren't helping, whatever Mum said. The second problem seemed easier, but still impossible: how to stop the row that was bound to happen when Mum called the council.

The bigger picture was how everything had changed since Grandad died. The two problems were like the yin-yang painting on Grandad's shed – different, but fitting together somehow. Both had happened because Grandad died. Could they be solved together?

If there was a huge, colossal row it might get Dad out of bed. He'd have to get involved in things again.

But that was no good. She had to *stop* the row so that she could keep her promise to Grandad.

If she took Dad to the allotment she might be able to persuade him to take her side and stop Mum calling Mr Thomas.

But there was no way she could get him out of bed.

It would take the strength of an elephant to drag him down there.

And then, suddenly, a vivid ray of sunshine pierced through the clouds, and the valley was illuminated in gold light. The eagles cried in triumph. *The strength of an elephant.* Kirsty had had a brilliant idea.

CHAPTER 24

'Wake up,' Kirsty whispered into Dawn's ear. It was tricky to stand on the bunk-bed ladder and hold a cup of tea and try to wake Dawn. She shook Dawn's shoulder. The tea – which was the colour of polished brown school shoes – spilled over on to the floor. 'Rats.'

'Wha' matta',' Dawn mumbled.

'Wake up. Tea for you.'

'Lea' me 'lone.'

Kirsty rolled Dawn over to face the day. 'Come on, it's morning. Time to get up.'

Dawn's angry T-rex glare nearly stopped Kirsty, but not quite. It was pretty scary, but Kirsty felt way too excited to stop. She shoved the cup towards Dawn, who took it with a scowl. She slurped at it, then coughed. 'Yuck! That's stronger than the Incredible Hulk.'

'Are you awake yet?'

'God, I hate sharing a room with you. You're like an evil alarm clock. What time is it anyway?'

Kirsty grinned. 'Er, quarter to seven.'

'What?' Dawn shoved the cup back at Kirsty. 'I don't believe you! Go away. Scram. Vamoose. It's Saturday. Let me sleep.'

'No, come on, Dawn. I need to speak to you. I've had a brilliant idea.'

'I don't listen to brilliant ideas before ten o'clock at the weekend.' Dawn threw the covers over her head and crawled down into the warm bed. Kirsty sipped at the tea. Dawn was right. It was horrible. She left to go and wake Ben.

The front room was in darkness, but Kirsty could tell from the moment she opened the door that he was awake. He was breathing quietly, not the regular deep sound of sleep. He had his grey duvet pulled high up over his head.

'Morning,' Kirsty whispered.

'Hello.' Ben's reply was dull and flat, as though he were speaking from far away. Kirsty let her eyes get used to the murky dark, then stepped inside. At the weekend, the front room became a tangle of clothes and books as Ben spread out. Kirsty was careful not to trip over the draught excluder or tread on any of the more radioactive-smelling socks.

'I'm glad you're awake,' she said. 'Dawn won't wake up and I need to talk to you both.'

'You tried to wake her? That's practically a suicide attempt.'

Kirsty sat down on the edge of his bed. It creaked in protest at the extra weight. 'Why are you awake?'

Ben turned to look at her. 'I couldn't sleep. Bad dreams.' He paused. 'I dreamt about Grandad. But it wasn't really Grandad, it was Dad and Dad was the one who died. And when I woke up it didn't really feel better, because in a way that's what it's like, isn't it? As though Dad's . . .' Ben's voice faded to a whisper.

Kirsty nodded slowly. 'Yes, it is a bit like that. I miss Dad.' She smiled suddenly. 'But I think I know what to do about it. That's why I was trying to wake Dawn. Come on, get up. You'll have to help me wake her up.'

'OK. Just pass me my suit of armour, will you?'

'She's your sister, not a dragon.'

'At seven o'clock in the morning, there's no difference.'

Ten minutes later, Dawn was propped up in bed like a hospital patient. Her face was creased with pillow marks and she looked furious.

'I swear, as soon as I can be bothered to get up out of this bed, you two are toast,' she said.

Kirsty grinned at her. 'Morning! I've had a great idea. I wanted to tell you about it before Mum and Dad get up. Well, Mum, anyway.'

Dawn's eyes narrowed. 'OK, you have thirty seconds and then I'm going back to sleep. This had better be good. Remember, your life is in danger.'

Kirsty took a deep breath. She was like the sultan's wife in the *Arabian Nights*, talking for her life, telling stories to avoid the cruel fate of the sultan's other, slaughtered wives. The executioner was only metres away, sharpening the blade. Only her words would save her now. She could almost feel the heat of the desert, the soft rustle of silk against her skin, the weight of the diadem on her head.

'Get on with it,' Dawn said. 'Twenty seconds left.'

'OK, OK. Like I said, I've had a great idea. It could solve everything. We'd get to keep the allotment and Dad would get better. But it's a risk. It's dangerous and we could get into trouble.'

'That doesn't sound great,' Ben said.

'Wait. I haven't got to the best bit.'

'Ten seconds.'

'We steal an elephant.'

There was a silence. Kirsty looked at both of them. Ben was wide-eyed with horror. Dawn was wide-eyed – at least she was awake now.

'We steal a *what*?' Dawn asked.

'An elephant. A stuffed elephant. From the museum.'

'*Why* exactly?' Ben said after another long pause.

Kirsty grinned. If he wanted to know why, then he wasn't saying no. At least not yet. 'Here's what I think. Dad doesn't think there's anything worth getting up for, right? It's almost as though he's fading away. He doesn't listen when you tell him things. He hardly notices you're there. He's not interested in *anything*. I think we have to *make* him interested again, whether he wants to be or not.'

'But why an elephant?' Ben asked blankly.

'It has to be something big! Something extraordinary!' How could she make them understand? 'It has to be something that really shakes everyone up, makes them pay attention. There's no way Dad can stay in bed if he knows his kids are out robbing museums! He'd really *notice* stuff again!'

'And – this is the best bit – if we steal from the museum, we'll get Mr Thomas's attention too. He loves the museum. His favourite gallery is Natural History. The woman at the desk told me so. And the stuffed elephant is the best thing there.'

'I suppose everyone's interested in a good crime. Especially one committed by your own children,' Dawn said nodding. 'But do you really think it will make a difference to Mr Thomas?'

'We've tried being nice and that didn't get us anywhere. We tried being cunning and that's going to get us grounded when Mum finds out. We have to get mean! If we kidnap something that Mr Thomas cares about, then he might listen. We can hold it to ransom.'

Dawn was nodding. 'Two birds with one stone. It's risky, but I like it.'

'Dawn!' Ben leapt up. 'You can't be serious! You must be still asleep! We can't steal an elephant. It's crazy! It's insane! It's impossible.'

'It's genius,' Dawn said. 'Consider it a challenge. Kirsty's right. Dad's like a zombie. We need to give him a shock to snap him out of it. And Mr Thomas will give us the allotment so that he can get the elephant back. He loves that museum. He'll be a hero. Everyone's happy. Don't worry, Ben. It will be fun.'

'But even if we could find a way to do it, do you really think it will work?'

Kirsty nodded. She was surer than she had ever been

before. 'This is the only thing that will work,' she said.

Ben bit his lip. Then he shrugged silently.

'Woo-hoo!' Kirsty punched the air. 'We're going to steal an elephant!'

CHAPTER 25

'I thought we could go to the park?' Mum said after breakfast. 'It's a bit chilly, but we can probably find the odd duck or three to feed.'

'Is Dad coming?' Ben asked quietly.

Mum shook her head, 'No. I don't think so, love.'

When Mum said that, Kirsty suddenly *knew* that what they were going to do was right. 'How about the museum?' she said. 'We haven't been there in ages.'

Dawn grinned wider than a Cheshire cat on its birthday. Ben seemed to shrink down further into his chair.

'Sure. The museum. Fine,' Mum said. 'If anyone needs the loo, go now. Everyone else, coats on.'

On a Saturday afternoon, with spring still hovering some way in the distance, the museum was full to bursting. Kirsty was amazed at the transformation. Two Mondays ago, when she had followed Mr Thomas, they had practically been the only people there. Today, it was as busy as an ants' nest, a big marble and cast-iron ants' nest. Kirsty looked up into the cavernous space of the ceiling. Today the air echoed with the shrieks of children, the chatter of adults, the tinny music coming from the headphones of the teenagers.

'Cool,' she said to no one in particular. Then she turned back to the others who were dithering at the cloakroom window. 'I'll fetch a map.'

Kirsty squeezed through the forest of bodies that had sprouted around the information desk. She ducked a handbag as it swung towards her head, then she swiped two leaflets from the desk. She stuffed one into the back pocket of her jeans, for use later. She twisted her way back out of the crowd and skipped towards the others. She unfolded the leaflet with a snap and then examined the map.

'Egypt, Natural History or Science? I think Natural History,' Kirsty said.

Mum smiled with more warmth than Kirsty had seen in days. 'Do you now? Don't the rest of us get any say?'

Kirsty smiled back. 'Nope.'

'Stuffed animals it is, then.'

Kirsty handed the map over to Mum, who led the way towards the archway at the end of the hall. Kirsty walked behind. Ben and Dawn came last. Ben held Dawn's elbow. 'Perhaps this isn't a good idea?'

'We're only looking at some dusty old animals.'

'No, we're not. We're, we're . . .' Ben thought hard for the right words. 'We're scoping the joint! That's what we're doing.'

'I don't know how to scope a joint. I'm just looking for a way to steal their elephant. And so is Kirsty, and so are you. And please let go of my arm in public. One of my friends might see you and think that I know you.'

Kirsty stopped and turned; she had been listening. She grinned at Ben. 'Don't worry. We're not going to steal it today, are we? Come on. I want to learn how to scope.'

The east wing of the museum building was devoted to stuffed animals, fossils, rocks, dried plants and old bones. In one case, shells and dried seaweed were strewn higgledy-piggledy, as though the glue keeping them in place had crumbled with age. In another case, rocks were lined up in neat rows, each marked with a label handwritten in a maze of spidery writing.

'Look at this, kids.' Mum had stopped in front of a

case. Inside, a stuffed owl glared at them with yellow eyes. Half a mouse hung from its beak, as though it had chosen exactly the wrong hole to bolt down.

'Yuck,' Kirsty said, looking at the mouse's stringy tail draped over the owl's beak.

'It's not "yuck", it's amazing,' Mum said. She drifted to the next case, which was filled with small birds glued to twigs.

'Oh, finches,' Mum said. 'Actually, these ones are a bit yuck. Their feathers look like they've been through the tumble drier too many times. They look so much better when they're alive. Though that goldfinch is beautiful.'

Kirsty caught Dawn's eye, then jerked her head dramatically towards the end of the gallery. The African savannah.

'Just going to look at the lions, Mum,' Kirsty called. Mum nodded without really listening. Kirsty led the way.

A group of animals stood on what was meant to be a typical savannah. Behind a low rope, a giraffe balanced on loose gravel, a lion lay in dried grass, a rhino guarded a plastic boulder and an elephant gazed out at a horizon of rocks and minerals in the next room.

'I bet they wouldn't be so happy together in real life,' Ben said glumly.

'They don't look very happy now,' Kirsty said.

It was true. The lion's mane looked grey with dust; the seam where the giraffe's neck had been sewn up was gaping gently. A small boy had slipped his arm under the rope and was throwing stones into the rhino's open mouth. He wasn't the first one to do this; the rhino's mouth was full of small stones, as though it had been grazing on the gravel.

Kirsty led the way round the group of animals until they were standing in front of the elephant. It was so noisy in the gallery, with shouts and gasps and crying babies, that they were able to talk without anyone overhearing.

'So, Ben. How do we scope a joint?' Kirsty asked.

Ben sighed. 'Well, in theory – and this is just In Theory, remember – you need to start with entrances and exits. How to gain access. Then security. Are there guards? Cameras? How can you get this out of here without anyone noticing? Then, of course, there's the big one. How are you planning on even moving the thing? In case you haven't noticed, it's massive.'

Kirsty gazed up into the tiny brown eyes of the elephant. They held such a deep, wise expression, that they reminded her a little bit of Grandad. Between his eyes, his trunk swept down to the ground. His ears hung like ragged grey bags at the sides of his face.

'He doesn't have tusks,' Kirsty said. 'Do you think that hunters took them?'

Ben looked up from the sign he had been reading. 'No. It never had tusks. It's not a *he*, it's a *she*. From Asia. They don't grow tusks.'

'Why's she in the African savannah?'

'She packed her trunk and went on holiday!' Dawn said with a huge grin.

Kirsty groaned and rolled her eyes. She stepped right up to the rope, as near as she could get to the animal without attracting attention from any security staff. She peered closer. 'She's hairy!'

'Is she?' said Ben. He leaned in to see the wiry sprouts of hair on her grey hide. 'You don't think of elephants as hairy, do you?'

Dawn sniffed contemptuously. 'All mammals have hair. Everyone knows that.'

'Even whales?' Ben asked.

'Er, yes, of course. Probably,' Dawn said, not sounding too sure.

Kirsty giggled. Dawn look huffy and stalked away.

Kirsty looked at the elephant. 'She *is* big, isn't she?' Kirsty said to Ben quietly.

Finally, Ben seemed to relax a little. 'Yes. Huge. Ginormous. It can't possibly be done.'

'But they got her in here in the first place, didn't

they? So it must be possible to get her out.' Kirsty grinned.

Ben's shoulders stiffened again.

'So, entrances and exits,' Kirsty said. She took the second leaflet from her back pocket and unfolded it to look at the map. 'There's the way we came in. She would fit under the archway but not out of the front doors, I don't think.'

Ben leaned in to take a closer look. 'Nope. It definitely won't go through the front doors. Oh well, we tried. Let's go now.'

'What about this?' Kirsty pointed to a grey rectangle drawn on one of the side walls of the building. '*"Goods lift – not for public use"*,' she read. 'Is that a real lift? It looks huge on this map.'

Ben sighed, then nodded. 'Yes, it will be a big lift.'

'On the map it looks like it goes down to street level. We should check it out. Dawn, look at this.'

Dawn was gazing up at the walls of the gallery. She came back and looked at the map. 'All right,' she said. 'Where's your mum?'

'Still over there by the dead little birds. Don't worry. Mum'll be happy for hours,' Kirsty said.

'Great. Let's go.'

There was a large alcove past the African savannah, about the size of a normal living room. The lift was set into the back wall. The whole area was crowded, but not with usual museum visitors. Men and women in black-and-white waiters' uniforms scurried around, unloading a lift so big that it looked like the inside of a lorry. They were bringing out some strange objects, mostly big metal boxes, but there were also huge, solid wooden wheels, taller than most of the people.

Kirsty, Ben and Dawn stared. Then Kirsty noticed a woman in uniform standing apart from the others. She was bent double with her hands on her knees, as though she had just come last in a really long race.

Kirsty went up to her and smiled. 'Excuse me, what's going on?'

'Banquet. Stuff. Tonight,' the woman wheezed. 'Asthma,' she added.

Kirsty nodded. Now she understood. She reached out towards one of the big wheels that rested against the nearest wall. 'Tables?' she asked.

The woman nodded but didn't speak; her lips were turning blue.

Kirsty's face crumpled in concern. 'Ben? This woman's lips are blue.'

'Wait,' Ben said. He looked around for someone who might be in charge. A man in a different uniform was standing to one side of the lift. He was wearing a grey jacket with black piping along the creases, with a radio clipped to his waist. He held a key which he had jammed into a panel by the lift. Ben walked over.

'Scuse me,' Ben said politely.

'Yes?' the security guard said.

'There's a woman over there with asthma. And blue lips. She's not well at all.'

The security guard looked across to the woman who was leaning heavily on Kirsty's shoulder.

'Blimey,' the man said and rushed over, grabbing for his radio as he went. Everyone was looking at the woman who had started wheezing noisily and clawing at the air. Ben's hand flashed up, pulled the key from its slot on the control panel and slipped it into his pocket without a soul noticing.

CHAPTER 26

'I can't believe I did it. I can't believe it,' Ben said, staring at the key in his palm as though it were a radioactive bomb. Kirsty grinned. He hadn't stopped talking like this since they had got home from the museum. He lifted the key nearer to his face and stared at its jagged teeth. 'I didn't even mean to. I don't even think this is a good idea. I think it's stupid. But my hand just did it, all by itself. Perhaps I was possessed?'

'Perhaps you just saw a good opportunity and took it. There's no need to get your knickers in a twist,' Dawn said. She stretched out on the top bunk, kicking her trainers on to the floor with a heavy thunk.

Kirsty reached over and snatched the key from his palm.

'Hey!' he said.

'What? You didn't want it anyway! I'm only having a

look.' Kirsty twisted the key around, peering at it from every angle. 'This is brilliant. Now we've got the key we can go in the middle of the night and take the lift up from the street. This is going to be easy.'

'Yes, dead easy. You've forgotten that they'll have alarms. And security guards. And then we have to move an *elephant*. Couldn't be easier. Couldn't be saner,' Ben muttered.

Kirsty chuckled. 'OK, I didn't mean easy. I meant not impossible. You're right about security. We got out of there so fast once you'd nicked the key, there wasn't time to check it out. We need to go back.'

Dawn started whistling. It was a drawled, aimless tune that was clearly meant to be irritating.

'What?' Ben asked grimly.

Dawn whistled louder.

'What?' Kirsty demanded.

'Well. While you two were staring like loons at the elephant, I was looking for cameras. I was working. In that gallery there was one CCTV camera on the balcony. It's pointing mostly at the giraffe, but it can probably see the elephant's back legs. There was also one of those boxes, like Mum has installed in the salon.'

'A sunbed?' Ben asked.

'No, you idiot. One of those little white boxes stuck

to the walls. An intruder alarm.'

Ben frowned. 'Do you reckon they have those laser beam things, like on films? You know, where you have to do gymnastics to cross the room without breaking a beam. Cos I can't do backflips.'

'No. Did you see their displays? They can't even afford glue to keep blue tits on their perch. I don't think we need to worry about lasers.'

Kirsty stood up, her eyes twinkling with anticipation. They were on the brink of a daring, cunning, extravagant plot. They just had to work out the finer details. 'Right,' she said. 'We haven't got much time. On Monday, Mum will contact a phone engineer. It will be fixed on Tuesday. That means that by Wednesday she'll have called the council; they'll all find out that Katy Jennings doesn't exist. And we'll all be grounded for life. So we need to act fast. Monday or Tuesday night at the latest. That gives us the rest of tonight and tomorrow to work out how to get past the security alarm, the camera and how to move an elephant. I think that Dawn should think about the alarm. Ben, you think about the camera, and I'll work on transport. Agreed?'

Dawn nodded her head vigorously, Ben nodded slowly. Kirsty clapped her hands – a signal for them all to get to work.

SUNDAY

CHAPTER 27

The house was unusually quiet on Sunday. Everyone was busy plotting.

Dawn lay sprawled on her bed with her sketchpad, scribbling and striking out, then scribbling again. Every time Kirsty tried to get into their room, Dawn threw pillows at her.

From the outside, Ben appeared less busy. He sat in the red car, watching a pair of starlings riffling through the dried leaves. But Kirsty knew that he was thinking hard – he hadn't started the engine once.

Kirsty left him alone and wandered into the living room. She sat down on the sofa. Her mind was chock-rammed-stuffed-full of the plan. Moving an elephant. An elephant. How on earth could they move an elephant? Could they go to a building site and hot-wire a JCB? Trundle it through the streets at night and drive it into the museum? Or go to the zoo and lure a live elephant out of its paddock with a trail of peanuts and get it to lift the stuffed one? Or assemble a team of circus strongmen to cart the elephant right out of the gallery?

Kirsty shook her head. All of those things would be brilliant fun, but they weren't quite right somehow. And she didn't have a clue how to make them happen. How heavy was a stuffed elephant anyway? What was it actually stuffed with? She had no idea.

Mum was in the kitchen chopping and mixing lard balls for the bird feeders. Dad was still in his room. 'Mum,' Kirsty yelled in the direction of the kitchen. 'Mum, what are stuffed animals stuffed with?'

'You mean like we saw yesterday? I haven't a clue. Ask your dad. Oh no. Best leave him be. Ask a teacher tomorrow.'

Kirsty sighed. Tomorrow was too late. She needed to know right now. Who would know? She could go back to the museum and ask, but that might seem suspicious. Kirsty grinned suddenly. Of course! The internet would know.

The computer was in the front room. During the week, it usually hummed quietly in the background and she would use it to search for more films for her collection. But at the weekend, when the front room became Ben's bedroom, the computer was switched off. She pulled one of Ben's T-shirts off the monitor and an odd sock off the keyboard, then switched it on.

She sat down and started tapping questions into Google. How much did an elephant weigh? Blimey. As much as a truck. What about a dead elephant? Still as much as a truck. A stuffed elephant? Brilliant! Light as a feather. Oh no, wait. That was toy elephants. There must be a website somewhere that knew the answer. She just needed to find it. She searched 'moving museum elephants'. Was there a company that did that? There! Arkwright's Museum Movers. '*Promising safe transport of all kinds of museum exhibits: jewellery, art, furniture, mummies, stuffed animals.*' Kirsty scrolled down. There was a price list with weights!

A stuffed song thrush, 20 grams: £30
A stuffed tiger, up to 70 kilos: £120
Anything larger than a tiger: price on application

Kirsty gulped. A tiger was tiny compared to an elephant. It might weigh hundreds of kilos! How on earth could they move it?

If only the elephant had its own wheels, then it wouldn't matter what it weighed, they could just push it along. An elephant on rollerblades, that's what they needed. Kirsty smiled slowly. Then an elephant on rollerblades was exactly what they would have. She switched off the computer. She had people to see.

Kirsty walked out past the broken cars. Ben was still leaning on the steering wheel, watching the birds. She knocked at the window. Ben leaned over and wound it down.

'What?' he said.

'I've had a great idea.'

'Please don't tell me.'

'Why not?'

'I've been thinking. I don't reckon we should be doing this.'

'But . . . Ben, you . . .'

'Oh, I'm not saying I won't do it. I just don't think it's right. So, if I only take charge of the camera, if Dawn only knows about the alarm and if you just work on moving the elephant, and none of us knows what the others are doing, then it's like we're not really planning it. Do you see? We're not really guilty.'

Kirsty frowned. 'I get what you mean. But I don't think you're right. First, I don't feel guilty. We're not going to hurt anyone. Second, just because you don't know exactly what I plan to do, you do know that I'm planning it.'

Ben shook his head. 'It just has to be this way, OK? So don't tell me anything.'

'You really don't want to know? Not even if my idea is so brilliant that you'll have to worship my genius for ever?'

'Not even then.'

'Suit yourself,' Kirsty said, and she strolled out on to the street.

CHAPTER 28

Kirsty walked away from the house towards the tower block that stood on the edge of the estate. The streets were quiet, but as she got closer she could hear the clatter and scrape of the boys practising on their skateboards. Good – they were there. She turned the corner at the end of the terrace. Now she could see the tower block before her. It stood by itself, with just the warehouses and the sea beyond. Today, the concrete space in front of the tower was full of boys of all different ages, flipping their boards, jumping plastic crates, falling, laughing, then doing it all again. The boy she was looking for sat on the steps in front of the entrance.

'Hi, Danny,' Kirsty said. 'Whatcha doing?'

Danny raised his eyes slowly, taking in her cheerful grin. 'Are you after something?' he said.

'No. Well, yes. I thought we could say hello and stuff first though.'

Danny shrugged. 'Hello.'

Kirsty sat down on the cold step next to him. His skateboard was on the step below. 'Is that yours?' Kirsty asked.

'Yes. Why?'

'It's nice.'

'What are you after? It's not lessons, is it?'

'No. But I do need a favour.'

Danny pulled his hood up and seemed to slide deeper into his clothes.

'I just want to borrow your skateboard. Well, four skateboards,' Kirsty said.

'Four? What do you need four for?'

'I can't tell you. But don't worry, I won't hurt them. I won't even ride them.'

'Then what do you want them for?'

'I can't say.'

'Is it against the law?'

'Yes.'

'Cool.'

'So, can I borrow them then?'

'What do I get out of it?'

'I'll do all your English homework for two months.'

'What if you get caught?'

'Then having your English homework will give me something to do in jail.'

'OK. It's a deal.'

Kirsty stayed on the step while Danny went to speak to the older boys. They muttered to each other, then they did a complicated handshake, holding wrists and slapping knuckles. She would have to get Ben to teach her that later. Finally, a few of the boys went indoors and came out carrying their spare boards. Within a few minutes, she had the four boards lined up in front of her. This was fantastic. With a few simple modifications, she would soon have a set of elephant roller-blades! There was rope in Grandad's shed. She could do it there.

'I need to take these down to the Jubilee Street allotments. Can you help?' she asked Danny.

He grinned at her. 'Do you think you can stay on one of those?'

'Yes. Easy,' she said, stepping on.

'Hold tight, then.'

Danny grabbed Kirsty's hand and one of the spare skateboards; another boy grabbed her other hand and another board. Suddenly, they were whizzing down the street. A third boy, with the last board under his arm, sped behind them. She was hurtling along, the wind whipping her hair, the wheels rumbling on tarmac under her feet. She leaned and bent into each corner. This was fun!

Too soon, they arrived at the allotments, the boys grinning and out of breath, Kirsty wobbly-legged, but filled with excitement.

'Thanks!' she said. 'Actually, Danny, when this is done, can I have a lesson?'

Danny smiled back. 'OK. But you'll have to do my maths homework too.'

By the time she'd finished with the boards and the bits of rope, the sky was beginning to turn dark blue. It would be night-time soon. She stretched and felt the muscles loosen in her arms and legs. It had been a great day's work. She had attached a coil of rope to the front of each board with gaffer tape, then attached a longer length to the back to tie like ballet shoes: part elephant ballet shoes, part elephant roller skates – elephant baller skates!

Kirsty tidied everything up in the shed then headed home. The streets were quiet in the growing dusk, just right for thinking things through as she walked. They had the key to get them into the lift. They had transport for the elephant. The phone would be fixed on Tuesday. Mum would phone Mr Thomas on

Wednesday. They didn't have much time. But Ben was clever and Dawn was determined; she was sure they would have worked out how to get past the security. They had to. Otherwise it was all over.

She could hear Dawn and Ben arguing in the front room as soon as she reached her house.

'No, you're the idiot!' Dawn yelled.

'Don't call me that. You're the one who wants to do this. We're going to get into big trouble.'

'Don't be such a baby.'

Kirsty put her key into the lock and stepped into the hall. Ben and Dawn stood in the middle of the front room, glaring at each other. They hardly noticed when Kirsty walked in. 'What's going on?' she asked.

'I'm not being a baby. I'm being sensible,' Ben yelled. 'Like you should be. If you weren't so thick, you'd see that.'

Dawn looked furious; her fists were clenched and she moved forward menacingly.

'Take that back,' she said.

'No. You are thick.'

'Arggh!' Dawn launched herself at Ben, knocking him to the floor. He pushed back and they rolled together, banging into the camp bed. Dawn struggled to pin Ben down. Ben thrashed his arms and legs.

'Stop it!' Kirsty rushed forwards and grabbed Dawn's

pullover, but it was no use. She wasn't strong enough to shift Dawn when she was in a rage.

'What on earth is going on in here?' Mum marched into the room.

There was a sudden silence. Dawn stopped pushing. Ben froze. Kirsty stepped back.

'Dawn, leave your brother alone. You should be ashamed of yourself. Someone had better tell me exactly what's going on here.'

Dawn pouted but didn't speak.

'She started it!' Ben said.

Dawn swiped at Ben, catching his shoulder with a thump.

'Right!' Mum said. 'You're both old enough to know better. Dawn, up to your room. Ben, you stay in here. Wait till your father hears about this.'

'Like he cares,' Dawn muttered, but not quietly enough.

'Upstairs. Now!' Mum snapped.

Dawn stomped out of the room. Kirsty felt herself being shepherded out by Mum. The door closed on Ben. Mum stalked back to the living room.

Kirsty was in the hallway alone. She sat down on the bottom stair. This was awful. Dawn could stay angry for days, and she could hold a grudge for even longer. Ben knew that. Was he deliberately trying to ruin the plan?

Kirsty felt cold at the thought. He wouldn't do that, would he? Although, even if he hadn't meant to, the plan was falling apart. She couldn't do it without Dawn and Ben, and now they weren't talking to each other. She put her chin in her hands. Time was running out.

'There is absolutely no way that I'm going to speak to him until he apologises for calling me thick,' Dawn said.

Kirsty pulled herself up the ladder so that she could look at Dawn. 'But, Dawn, it's really important. You two will be gone in the morning. We need to sort this out before you go.'

'It will be sorted, as soon as he says sorry.' Dawn put her headphones in her ears and closed her eyes. As far as she was concerned, the conversation was over.

Kirsty felt her own temper rising. Dawn was so annoying! There was no one in the world who could be so stubborn. She was impossible. Kirsty got down off the bunk bed. Perhaps Ben would be easier.

'There's no way I'm going to say sorry to her. She hit me!'

'But you did call her names.'

'She deserved it.'

'But, Ben, if you don't speak to her this will ruin

everything. Is that what you want?'

Ben didn't speak. He looked at the ground.

Kirsty felt the cold feeling again. He *did* want to ruin it! It *was* what he wanted! She was sure of it. He was going to let her down. He was going to let Grandad down. She felt tears burn her eyes. 'I can't believe you're backing out. You've helped me so much. You can't stop now.'

Ben still said nothing.

Kirsty stared hard into his face. He looked sad and uncomfortable, but certain. 'It's funny,' she said. 'I always thought of Dawn as my half-sister. But you were always my brother – it was that simple. Now, I guess you are only my half-brother.'

Ben looked shocked, but Kirsty didn't stay to wait for an answer. She ran out of his room, up the stairs and into the bathroom. With the door locked behind her, she sat on the floor, her forehead against the cold enamel of the bath. She had never felt so alone.

MONDAY

CHAPTER 29

Kirsty couldn't sleep. She lay in the dark, listening to the house creak and groan. Strange, disturbing noises kept her awake: doors squeaked open, floorboards moaned, an eerie tapping came from somewhere nearby, like skeleton fingers picking the locks. Kirsty pulled the duvet up right over her face. It was hot and hard to breathe, but it felt safer. She shivered despite the heat and wished that the daytime would come.

When the alarm clock rang, she felt crotchety. Perhaps this was how Dawn felt every morning. Kirsty didn't want to speak to anyone, especially not Dawn or Ben. Not after they'd ruined everything with their stupid row. She went downstairs. Mum was up already. She could hear Ben moving in the front room. The stairs creaked. Dawn was following her down.

'Morning, girls,' Mum said. Neither of them answered. 'Oh, it's one of those mornings, is it? Well, I've got a message for you. Ben wants you to go into the front garden.'

Kirsty frowned. 'Why?'

'I don't know. But he told me to tell you it's important. You've both got your slippers on – go and look.'

Kirsty opened the front door. The cold morning air blew away all the last traces of sleep. She looked around the garden and gasped. Behind her, she heard Dawn laugh.

Next to the red car, the broken down grey car had had an overnight transformation. The front doors were open and draped in grey pillowcases, like ears flapping in the breeze; two circles of paper for eyes were stuck on to the windscreen; below the eyes a long, draft-excluder trunk curled gracefully down the bonnet. Ben had turned the car into an elephant! Dawn was laughing properly now. Kirsty was soon giggling too. The elephant-car looked so funny. She looked towards the front room window. Ben stood there, grinning nervously. He held up a piece of card with 'Sorry' scribbled on it.

'That's the best apology ever,' Dawn said.

'Yes. Come on, let's get breakfast. We've got loads to do today if the plan's back on!'

In between washing, getting dressed and eating break-fast, they managed to snatch a few minutes to talk while Mum sorted out packed lunches.

'The transport is sorted,' Kirsty said firmly.

'I can disable the alarm,' Dawn said.

They both looked at Ben. He still seemed quiet, even after his apology. Kirsty remembered what she had said to him last night and felt her own twinge of guilt.

'Well?' Dawn said, still looking at Ben.

'I can get us past the camera. But I'll need to go to the museum after school today to be completely sure.'

'So we'll all be ready tomorrow?' Dawn asked.

'Yes. And the phone's being fixed then, so we have to steal it tomorrow,' Kirsty said. 'Do you want to meet later today?'

Ben shook his head. 'No, my visit to the museum could take a while. We'll meet outside the museum tomorrow, before it closes. And we'll go through the plan then. Tell your mum you're staying the night with us. We'll tell our mum we're sleeping here. Then we'll be ready to break in tomorrow night.'

Dawn nodded firmly, then walked towards the front door. Ben turned to follow. Kirsty grabbed his arm and whispered quickly, 'I'm sorry I said you were only my half-brother. I didn't mean it really.'

Ben smiled properly for the first time all morning. 'Thanks.'

CHAPTER 30

There was the rest of Monday to get through. Kirsty fizzed with excitement all day. It was worse than waiting for her birthday! After school she went to the allotments. It was quiet – hardly anyone was about. She headed towards the brightly painted shed that stood out among the regular brown sheds like a peacock in a flock of pigeons. She walked along the main path and on to the allotment. Someone was there already. Someone sitting with their back to her. Dad. She gasped, her hand covering her mouth to stifle the noise. But it was too late; she had been noticed. He stood up, knocking over the upturned bucket he had been sitting on. Its metal handle clanged noisily on the hard earth. 'Kirsty!'

He looked pale. Over the past few weeks, Kirsty had only seen him in the semi-darkness of his bedroom.

Outside, his skin seemed almost transparent, except where his stubble had thickened into a beard.

Kirsty smiled warily. 'Hi, Dad.'

He leaned over to pick up the bucket, then sat down again without saying anything. Kirsty walked towards him slowly. 'Dad? Are you OK?' He stared out at the allotment, his face as cold and still as the earth below them.

Suddenly, he spoke. 'Do you know how long your grandad had this allotment?'

'Er, no.'

Dad frowned, the lines on the sides of his mouth deepening. 'Since I was a little boy. Forty years, at least.'

Kirsty waited for him to carry on, but he didn't. 'Dad, what are you *doing* here?'

'I don't know.'

'Are you feeling better?'

'Better? No. Not really.'

'But you're outside. That's good.'

'Is it?' Dad covered his eyes with the tips of his fingers, as though the light was hurting them. 'It was a mistake to come here. This isn't your grandad's now. He's gone.'

'Do you think so?' Kirsty hated hearing Dad sound so sad. 'I think this is where he is the most.'

'He's gone, Kirsty. He's never coming back. Look at the state of those beds. Weeds poking up already and it's not even spring properly. Nothing planted. Nothing bought in to even start planting. It's only been a few weeks since he died and look at the state of it. He's not here, is he? We can't even pretend.' Dad's voice was soft. He didn't cry, didn't sound angry.

Dad stood up. His body seemed frail and frozen. He moved with too much care. He moved like Grandad.

'We could plant stuff!' Kirsty said quickly.

'What would be the point?' Dad moved towards the main path.

'Where are you going, Dad?'

'Home. I'm tired now.'

'Do you want me to come with you?'

'No, you stay. Say goodbye. There'll be a new tenant here soon enough.'

Kirsty shivered. His voice frightened her. She didn't dare speak. Dad was getting worse. They had to go through with the plan for his sake, as well as Grandad's. They needed to make him see that there was a point to carrying on. But would it work? Kirsty let Dad walk away. It was a long time before she was ready to head for home.

TUESDAY

CHAPTER 31

If the wait on Monday had been bad, on Tuesday it was much worse. She had to go to school, but the lessons were like irritating insects buzzing around her head. All she could think about was the elephant.

As soon as the end-of-day bell rang, Kirsty grabbed her bike and dashed towards the town centre. She rattled her way over the cobbled street that led down to the oldest part of the town. She skidded to a halt in front of the cathedral. There was a bike rack just to the side of the main entrance. Once her bike was locked, she skipped over to the museum steps. The carved and blackened stone front of the museum towered over her. She sat down to wait. A few minutes later, Dawn and Ben arrived. Dawn clutched her huge school bag to her side with both hands, as though she was frightened that it would fly away. Ben looked twitchy and scared.

'Hello!' Kirsty said cheerfully.

Dawn grinned back. Ben just nodded.

'So, let's go through the plan,' Kirsty said. 'The transport is in Grandad's shed. The elephant is just going to roll out of the museum! I'll go and get everything from the allotment before tonight. We'll get in through the goods lift. What about the alarm and the CCTV camera?' Kirsty asked.

'I have to disable the alarm now from inside,' Dawn said.

'And I have to disable the camera too,' Ben said.

'Cool. So we knock out the alarm and the camera now. Then we go to the shed to wait until everyone is asleep. Then we come back here. How about eleven o'clock?'

Dawn laughed. 'Not eleven! Things like this have to be done exactly at midnight. It's kind of the rules.'

'Midnight, then. Perfect. How are you going to disable the alarm?'

Dawn held up her school bag, which seemed to be stuffed fuller than usual. 'Plan A,' she said. 'Do you want to shock and horrify a few people?'

Kirsty smiled. 'I could give it a try. What do I have to do?'

Dawn opened her bag, then grabbed wildly. A red balloon, filled to bursting with helium, tried hard to float out of her grasp. 'You just have to help me up the stairs. I can't do it alone in my condition.' Dawn shoved the balloon up her jumper. Her school uniform stretched across her middle, as though she were pregnant. It looked very uncomfortable. 'We have to get this into the Africa gallery. And, by the way, we can't stuff this up – there isn't a Plan B.'

'No problem,' Kirsty said and obediently held out her arm.

Dawn leaned heavily on Kirsty as they walked up the steps. Ben followed behind, his face glowing red with embarrassment. Dawn struggled through the revolving doors – they were old-fashioned and very narrow, designed for people a lot thinner. The main hall was quiet again after the noisy crowds at the weekend. There were only two people there: the lady behind the information desk and a security guard who leaned up against it, chatting as though it were a neighbourly fence between them. The security guard's jaw fell open. Kirsty tried to stop herself grinning but it was so hard. Dawn sighed heavily and put her hand to the base of her spine as though it was sore. The lady behind the desk prodded the guard to stop him staring. Kirsty smothered a giggle. Together they hobbled towards the Africa gallery. The sad troupe of savannah animals huddled tight together as though they were waiting to board Noah's Ark.

'That was brilliant!' Dawn said. 'Did you see their faces?'

'Awesome,' Kirsty agreed.

Dawn pulled the balloon out from under her top.

'What's going to happen when you let it go?' Kirsty asked.

'Well. Nothing yet. But when they come to turn on the alarm tonight, they'll find that this gallery registers an intruder. The motion sensor will go off. And when they come to investigate, they'll see that the culprit is this little balloon, bobbing around the ceiling. And they won't be able to get it down, so they won't be able to set the alarm. Simple, but incredibly clever.'

'Cool,' Kirsty said. Dawn held up her hands and let the balloon float gently up towards the high, high ceiling two floors above. She watched it bob against the pale blue plaster work, as though it were free in the sky.

'Lovely,' Kirsty said. She turned to Ben. 'What's the plan for the camera?'

He rummaged in his own school bag and pulled something out. 'This.'

'What's that?' Kirsty asked. Ben was holding what used to be a wire coat hanger. It was now pulled into a narrow rectangle. The hook extended from one of the short edges of the rectangle – it looked like a skeletal arm, with a hook for a hand. A small piece of card was taped to the other end, where a shoulder might be.

'I've not got a name for it yet. Maybe Ben's Brilliant Idea, or Ben's Blinking Awful Plan. I guess I'll wait to see if it works out before I name it.'

'Yes,' said Kirsty patiently. 'But what is it?'

'Come on, I'll show you.'

They moved out of the Africa gallery, back towards the sweeping staircase that led upstairs. On the first floor, Ben steered them on to the balcony that looked down over the stuffed animals. If they peered between the bars, they could see the security camera screwed to the bottom edge of the balcony.

'What time is it?' Ben whispered.

'Museum closes in ten minutes,' Dawn said, looking at her watch.

'Should be OK,' Ben said grimly. He glanced about him. The whole first floor seemed deserted. He dropped down on to his knees. 'Keep watch for me.' He slid the old coat hanger between the bars.

'Oh, it's a photo!' Kirsty said.

'Yes, I came in and took it yesterday.'

The small piece of card at the end of the contraption was a photograph of the gallery that they were looking down on. It was taken from exactly where they stood,

213

showing exactly the same view that they were looking at: the giraffe and the back end of the elephant.

Ben adjusted the hook, then took one quick look around. He leaned forwards and slipped the hook over the back of the camera, so that the photo hung in front of the lens. The camera whirred slightly as it auto-focused.

'Done. Now when they look, they'll just see an empty room, which is the way it should be as soon as the museum closes,' Ben said in a heavy voice.

'Brilliant!' Kirsty said loudly. 'You two are geniuses.'

'Shh,' said Dawn, grinning. 'Let's try not to draw attention to ourselves as we plan a robbery.'

'Good point.'

'So, the alarm is out. The camera is sorted. Shall we go and check the transport?'

'Before we leave, we should also check the primary access point for obstructions,' Ben said.

'What?'

Ben sighed. 'I mean, let's go outside and make sure no one has parked in front of the goods lift.' He shoved his school bag at Dawn. 'Here, put this up your jumper, or they'll come looking for a baby in here.'

They slipped quietly out of the museum and down the steps. According to the map, the goods lift was set in the east wall, which was around to the right. The museum was made of huge blocks of sandstone, dark as puddle water. Kirsty dragged her palm along the stone as she walked. If she ever had a castle, this was the kind of stone she'd build it out of. They followed the wall as it turned the corner.

The road narrowed into an alley, with cobbled stones beneath their feet. Shadows sprawled on either side of them. Kirsty heard a sudden scurrying noise in the gloom. Rats? She smothered a squeal. Above them, the evening sky was darkening. A street lamp buzzed into life at the far end of the alley. Suddenly, the wall they were following dipped into an alcove. They could just make out the garage-door shape of the lift in the darkness. Ben took out his phone and held the bright screen up to give them light.

'OK,' Kirsty said. 'Nothing in the way. We should be able to get the elephant through here.'

'Oh no,' Ben said. 'Not good.'

'What?' Kirsty asked.

'Not good at all. Look!' He shone his phone along the edges of the lift where it met the wall. The beam of light inched up one side, across the top and then back down the other side.

'I don't see anything,' Dawn said.

'Exactly. There's nothing there. There's no key hole to operate the lift. You can't open the lift door from the street. You have to be inside the museum.'

No one answered. Kirsty heard the faint sound of traffic in the distance, dulled by the sound of the blood rushing in her ears as she realised what needed to be done.

'I'll hide inside,' she whispered.

'No!' Dawn and Ben said together.

'I have to, don't I? This is my idea. And I'm the smallest. I can find somewhere to hide much easier than either of you. I have to . . .' Kirsty's voice trailed off quietly.

She looked at Ben. His eyes glistened in the darkness and his mouth was pulled into a hard line.

'She's right,' Dawn said. She looked worried too, but from the firm set of her eyebrows, Kirsty could tell that Dawn realised it was the only way.

'I need the key,' Kirsty said. She held out her hand to Ben. He slipped it slowly from his pocket and laid it in her palm.

'You'll need other things too. Food, water, stuff like that. Ben, look in your school bag. Give her anything useful.' Dawn started pulling things out of her own bag and shoving them at Kirsty. Her sketchbook, a tube of mascara, some tissues, her iPod. Ben pushed his water bottle and lunch box into Kirsty's open bag.

'What about my bike? If I leave it out the front,

they'll be suspicious.'

'We'll take it to the shed when we pick up the transport.'

'Fine. You can't miss them. They're the weirdest things in the shed. Let's do this.'

At the bottom of the steps, Kirsty unlocked her bike. She slipped the lock into her bag and let Ben take hold of the handlebars.

Dawn checked her watch. 'You have to hurry. The museum's closing in a few minutes. Find somewhere good to hide. Then at midnight exactly, open the lift. We'll be waiting. Go on. Good luck.'

Kirsty turned away and ran. She rushed up the steps and stopped for a moment. She looked out towards the town, where traffic crawled under orange lamps. She felt scared now; her heart beat so hard it was as though someone were using a sink plunger inside her chest. She took a deep breath and stepped back into the museum building.

CHAPTER 32

In the entrance hall, the security guard was talking to the lady at the information desk again. Neither of them noticed Kirsty. She sidled into the Africa gallery. Where could she hide? Glass cabinets backed up against the walls; there was no room behind those. The exhibits in the middle of the room were way too open; there was nowhere to hide among those either. Think, think. There! A modern wooden bench, a bit like a church pew designed by IKEA, leaned up against the wall. It had a tall back and the section between the seat and the floor was boxed in, but it had no side panels. Just big enough for her and her bulging school bag. Kirsty grinned, then looked around quickly before ducking down into the hollow space. It was a good job that Ben's photo hung in front of the camera. It meant that no one had even seen her come in.

The space that she found herself in was low and narrow. She couldn't sit up. She lay on her side with her knees pulled up towards her chest. She tried to make her body relax. It was difficult. It was dark and uncomfortable, with wooden panels on either side of her. She could smell the dust, and small balls of grey fluff had gathered in the corners. She gasped; it was almost like being inside a coffin! Was she really going to stay here until midnight?

Dong! Dong! Dong! An old-fashioned school bell rang in the distance.

'Closing time. Closing time.' The shout echoed through the empty halls.

Kirsty held her breath and pulled her knees up closer to muffle the sound of her heart beating. This was it!

A few moments later she heard the stern clip of heavy soles on the stone floor. A radio crackled into life. 'This is Charlie One. Gallery 10 is clear. Over,' a man's voice said.

He spoke like a policeman. Kirsty bet he wore a smart uniform and black shoes so polished you could see your face in them. She wanted to take a peek at him, but she knew that if she made the slightest noise she would ruin everything. She stayed frozen still until the shoes clipped away again. Then a heavy clunk, and the lights went out. Kirsty gasped. She hadn't planned on being crouched in her coffin-shaped space until midnight *in the dark*. She felt her skin crawl as she imagined the mummies lying upstairs, the gravestones and urns and skeletons dotted around the vast, black museum halls. It was as though clawed fingers were walking slowly up her spine. She clamped her hand over her mouth to stop herself screaming.

Then, a small fizzing sound; the open ends of the seat were filled with a pale blue light. It wasn't bright, just enough to see shapes, but not colours. Kirsty crawled forwards slowly and edged her head out enough to peek into the gallery. High above, on the ceiling, two small lights were on, like the emergency lights in the corridors at school. She sighed in relief; at least she wasn't going to be totally terrified all night.

She crawled back into the dim space. She was going to have a long wait until midnight. Kirsty tried to read the dial on her watch. The hands were impossible to see. But she knew it wasn't anywhere near midnight yet.

Her school bag was wedged into the space by her shoulders, with Ben's lunch box inside. It was as good a time as any to see what was for tea. She unzipped it; the sound of the teeth springing apart sounded way too loud in the darkness. Kirsty prized off the lid and her hiding place filled with the cheesy smell of old butty-boxes. It was horrible, but her stomach rumbled anyway. She groped inside the container. There was an apple; she could feel its waxy skin beneath her fingertips and, yuck, the squelchy part where he had taken a bite before putting it back in the box. Revolting. She could also feel a few crusts. They had been hardening all afternoon so that now they were like cold toast. She put back the lid in disgust.

Clip, clip, clip. Someone was coming! The footsteps trotted in the same precise march that she had heard earlier. Charlie One! He was coming this way! She froze. She heard him speak into his radio, but he was too far away for her to make out the words. The footsteps came closer. Was he in the Africa gallery?

'This is Charlie One, 6 p.m. check on Galleries 1 through 10 complete. All clear. Set the alarm. Over.'

The radio crackled with static and a tinny voice answered, 'Roger that, Charlie One. I've just put the kettle on. Fancy a brew? Over.'

'Affirmative. There's some HobNobs in my locker. Over.'

The footsteps retreated.

They were ready to set the alarm. The gallery was still and quiet. Kirsty tried to keep as motionless as the stuffed animals around her. The minutes trickled away painfully slowly. Then Kirsty heard Charlie One's footsteps. He was in the Africa gallery again. Why was he back? Had they spotted her? Did they suspect? She heard a dramatic sigh and the short static burst of the radio.

'Come in, Alpha One. This is Charlie One. It's a ruddy balloon in Gallery 10. Some kid must have lost it. It's up on the ceiling now. Shall I come and get the air rifle? Over.'

'No, Charlie One. You know what a fuss Dr Livingstone made about the holes in the plaster last time.' There was a pause. Kirsty strained to hear. Alpha One spoke again. 'Best just leave it, Charlie One. It'll come down of its own accord tomorrow. I won't set the internal gallery alarm. We'll still have the alarms on all the external doors. We can do hourly checks instead. Come on, your tea's getting cold. Over.'

Charlie One's shoes squeaked on the stone floor as he turned and left the gallery.

Kirsty stayed completely still until her left leg began to tingle with numbness. But there were bigger things to think about than her legs. The alarm in the rooms was off, but the exit door alarms were still on! Dawn had assumed that all the alarms were on the same circuit – that if you couldn't set one, then you couldn't set any of them. But she had been wrong! It was fine to wander around the galleries, but the minute Kirsty turned the key and opened the lift doors the alarms would ring through the whole museum! And, to make things worse, Charlie One would be clip-clopping his way through the rooms every hour.

Kirsty felt a huge emptiness open up in her stomach. It wasn't hunger, or at least, it wasn't just hunger. It was fear. She was alone in the museum and she had only a few hours to come up with a plan to disable the alarm and keep the guards out of the Africa gallery. It was all up to her. If she failed, it all failed.

What could she do? She took a few deep breaths and tried to think. What if she sneaked out of her hiding place and locked the guard room? No, they were bound to have a phone in there; they could just call the police. Could she lock herself in the Africa gallery? They'd know something was up, but there might be time for them to steal the elephant. She sighed. No. As soon as the alarm went off, the guards would just come around the outside of the building, catch them red-handed and *still* call the police. What she needed was a diversion, a way of sending them off on a wild goose chase to the other end of the museum to give her time to sneak off with the elephant. But what? And how?

Kirsty twisted around in the cramped space until she found her school bag. There must be something in there she could use.

She felt inside: a water bottle, a sketchbook, tissues, a tube of mascara, her pencil case, an iPod, her bike lock and the lunch boxes. None of them turned into deadly gadgets. None of them launched missiles. None of them could be assembled into a super-intelligent robot. This was going to take a lot of thinking. Well, she had hours.

There were no windows in the gallery, so there was no moonlight or starlight marking the beginning of night. It would have been hard for Kirsty to judge how quickly the time passed, but Charlie One kept her straight. He patrolled the gallery every hour. The first time, at 7 p.m., Kirsty had been terrified of being spotted. But as the hours crept by, she became more used to his visits. He was like a scary cuckoo clock, popping out every hour.

In the quiet, dim light, between his visits, Kirsty thought about the diversion. What would keep Alpha and Charlie away from the Africa gallery, even when the alarm went off? An explosion? That would do the trick, but she had no idea how to make something explode. A strange noise to be investigated? That was more possible. She could definitely make a noise. In fact, she could even set off the alarm in a *different* gallery. That way they'd be investigating in the wrong place! She began to feel excited. That would work. She thought about all the galleries she knew in the building. Where should she send them to investigate? Oh yes. Kirsty grinned at the darkness. She knew the perfect place.

Now that she knew what she was going to do, the moments seemed to drag on endlessly. She fought hard to keep still and quiet. Charlie One had his eleven o'clock check to do before she could move. Finally, she heard his steps.

'Come in, Alpha One. Galleries 1 to 10 are completely fine. The animals are still stuffed. The mummies ain't moving. Can I come back now? Over.'

'Roger that. Fancy a game of backgammon? Over.'

'Lovely. Set it up. I'll beat you this time. It will be Game. Over.'

There was a chuckle and the steps receded.

Kirsty squirmed out of her hiding place. She whipped the black mascara wand across her cheeks, Apache-style. Then she grabbed her bag and stuffed everything into it. She was ready.

She walked swiftly across the Africa gallery. The camera here wouldn't spot her. It would be a different story in the rest of the museum. She took a deep breath before stepping into the next room. She hoped the guards were playing a long and interesting game of backgammon, with their backs to the CCTV screens.

She kept to the shadows. If she remembered the map properly, she had to cross the entire museum. Like a spy stealing through an enemy embassy, she crouched, she ducked, she crept, she slunk. The future of everything depended on the success of her mission. She had memorised the plan. She was Girl-Spy Extraordinaire. She reached the archway and the main hall opened up in its full marble splendour before her: white walls, glistening columns, pale ceiling, emergency lights that seemed to sparkle like chandeliers.

How could she cross this huge, light, open space? In her dark uniform, Alpha and Charlie couldn't fail to see her on the security cameras. What would Girl-Spy Extraordinaire do? Camouflage, that's what she needed. She had to be as pale as the walls around her. She looked in her school bag again. Dawn's sketchbook! There were loads of blank pages. She had some Sellotape in her pencil case. She tore out a few pages and stuck the edges together, then a few more, then a few more. Soon she had a white paper sheet just big enough to hide behind. She held it up, so that the pages touched the floor. Crab-like, she inched along the white wall. Every rustle of paper made her heart pound harder. Would they see her? Would they hear her? She was halfway across. Three-quarters. She was there! On the other side, she strained with every muscle to hear whether Charlie One was running to catch her. The hall stayed empty. She breathed out again. She left her paper sheet on the ground.

Beyond the main entrance, dark corridors stretched out into the opposite wing of the museum – dark arteries that she could creep through. She set off into the gloom.

The very last room at the end of the furthest corridor opened out before her. The Egypt gallery. The room where the mummies slept, their crumbling bodies shrouded in rotting bandages. Kirsty swallowed.

She stepped up to the doorway. Her foot moved reluctantly, as though it had a huge wodge of chewing gum sticking it to the floor. She could hear her own quick breathing. She was the only living thing within shouting distance – she hoped. Her eyes flashed around the room, noting objects and their positions. Eight coffins with mummies in. An open coffin in the centre of the room. *Ignore the mummies, ignore the mummies.* She couldn't. Their staring gold eyes seemed to glow with malice. She gave a small moan. She had to do this quickly so she could get out of here! She forced her eyes to move on. Where was the camera? There! Set into the wall above the emergency exit. Its steady lens gazed down, unblinking. She couldn't disable it; it was out of reach. This called for stealth and courage!

She took all the things she needed from her bag and then stashed it behind one of the entrance doors. The doors had handles – that would be useful later.

She checked her watch in the green light above the entrance. 11.50 p.m. Her heart lurched. Ten minutes left! It was time to set the trap.

She rushed into the room and crouched behind the coffin in the middle, which shielded her from the view of the camera.

Kirsty opened her packet of tissues and began tearing them into strips. When she had a small pile in front of her, she reached for the iPod. She knew Dawn had a creepy, whispering tune on there somewhere. She flicked until she found it, then hit the repeat button and turned the volume up full so it could be heard coming through the headphones. Finally, she looked at her lunch box, judging the width. She peered around the coffin edge, at the emergency exit. The box was about the same width as the gap between the push bar and the door. She took a deep breath. She was ready.

Kirsty tossed the iPod up into the air like a grenade. It landed inside the coffin. Now the muffled tune echoed off the coffin walls. It sounded terrifying, like something alive and moving.

She threw the strips of tissue after the iPod. They sailed over the coffin; some caught on the wooden edge, others floated to the ground.

She flung herself to the floor, then crawled, elbow over elbow, commando-style, towards the emergency exit, keeping to the shadows that spilled from the mummy cases. As soon as she was close enough, she leaned down heavily against the bar. It crashed open. Suddenly, the gallery filled with a cold breeze and the insistent wailing of an alarm. She struggled against the wind and managed to haul the door closed again. She jammed her empty butty-box under the bar. That would stop it opening again for a while! The wind died down but the alarm carried on ringing. They would be here any second! She had no time to lose. Kirsty pelted back to the entrance, then slipped behind the door where her bag – and her bike lock – were waiting.

In no time at all, she heard Charlie One's footsteps pounding down the corridor. He was breathing hard. His radio crackled and squawked, 'Report, Charlie One. Report. Is it a code 349? Over.'

'Give me a chance, Alpha,' Charlie One panted. 'I've only just got here. Over.'

He was standing right next to her. There was only the thin door separating Kirsty and Charlie One. She squeezed her eyes closed. *Please go inside, please go inside*, she thought, over and over.

Charlie One walked into the room. His steps were slow and reluctant. He paused.

'Come in, Alpha One. Over,' he whispered into his radio. His voice shook with a trace of panic.

'Go ahead. Over.'

'Exit 8 alarm activated. Probable suspect, a-a-a-mummy.'

'What?' Alpha One shouted.

'Shh. Repeat, a mummy on the move. Bandages on the floor,' his voice croaked. 'Strange whispering,' he whimpered. 'And it's freezing cold. They're alive! They're alive!'

Kirsty pushed hard against the door. It swung closed. She grabbed the other one and pushed that to. She could hear Charlie One running towards her inside the gallery. She whipped her bike lock through the handles and rammed it home. The door was locked tight.

Charlie One screamed into his radio, 'Alpha, help! It's got me trapped! It'll eat my brains and turn me into a zombie. Come and get me!'

'Don't panic, Charlie. I'm on my way.'

Kirsty picked up her bag and raced back along the corridor. That should keep security busy for a little while. Long enough for them to steal the elephant anyway. She hoped Dawn wouldn't be too angry about losing the iPod.

She crossed the hall quickly, not worrying this time about being seen. Alpha and Charlie were in exactly the wrong place for catching intruders.

In the Africa gallery, she checked her watch one last time. Midnight. T minus zero! She ran past the animals to the lift. She slid the key into the slot. She could just make out the whir of the lift engine beneath the roar of the alarm. The lift went down; she heard the doors scrape open, then the lift rose.

'Kirsty, why is the alarm ringing?' Ben said as he stepped out.

'Long story. Zombie mummies. Anyway, we have to hurry.'

'Let's go!' Dawn grinned. She held up two skateboards that had ropes flapping from them. Ben held two more.

Kirsty grabbed a skateboard from Dawn's hands and raced over to where the elephant towered mournfully above the rhinos. She jumped over the low rope and crouched by its front leg. 'Right, when I say three, everyone lift this leg up. Ready?' Ben and Dawn stepped over the rope and grabbed the elephant's knee. 'One, two, three!'

The elephant's leg wobbled into the air. Its body

lurched to the right, showering dust on to the rhino below. Kirsty jammed the skateboard under its foot. 'Down!' She tugged the front loop over its toenails, jamming it on tight. Then she laced the back rope around its ankle, lashing it firmly in place.

'And now the other legs,' Kirsty said. They worked quickly. Soon, the elephant was wearing four giant roller skates. Kirsty giggled, sure she could see a gleam of surprise in its brown eyes. She unhooked the barrier. 'One, two, three, push!' Slowly at first, but picking up speed, the elephant rolled forwards. Together they guided it along the smooth floor.

Kirsty kept one eye on the halls behind them. Had Alpha rescued Charlie One? 'Come on. We've got no time,' she said.

The goods lift was metres away. And then, Kirsty heard the unmistakable sound of someone running – and not too far away.

'Oh no,' she said. 'Alpha and Charlie are coming!'

Ben stopped heaving at the elephant's shaggy leg. 'Alpha and Charlie. Who are they?'

'Security! Come on!'

'What about Bravo?' Ben asked.

'What are you talking about?'

'Alpha, Bravo, Charlie. That's the police phonetic alphabet. If there's an A and a C, then where's B?'

Kirsty felt a sudden sinking sensation in her stomach. 'Perhaps he's got the night off?' she said.

'Let's get out of here. Now!' Dawn said. Kirsty turned the lift key and the doors shuddered open. With a heave they got the elephant in. There was just enough room for the three of them to cram themselves in too. Kirsty slammed the 'down' button with the palm of her hand. The lift seemed to crawl towards the street. When the doors finally opened the air felt suddenly cold against Kirsty's skin – they were out. And so was the elephant.

They pushed her out of the lift. The skateboards juddered over the cobbles. Somewhere outside in the darkness and not too far away Kirsty heard the crackle of a radio. 'Goods lift. Roger that.' And then footsteps running nearby and getting closer.

'There's a security guard out here!' Dawn said.

'I guess we've found Bravo,' Kirsty said.

'What are we going to do?' Ben asked.

'Run!'

CHAPTER 33

They ran. Ben and Dawn pushed the elephant's back legs; Kirsty stood between the front legs, gripping the knees to steer. It was like pushing a huge, hairy shopping trolley. At the end of the alley, the cobbles gave way to road. A car swerved to avoid them and its horn sounded loudly. The elephant picked up speed, gaining momentum until it seemed to be stampeding away from the museum.

'Did we lose him?'

'I can't see him.'

'Can you hear him?'

'I dunno, there's too much noise.'

'What is that noise?'

'Oh no. Sirens! Police!'

'Can they really know so soon?'

'It must have been the alarm. We have to move.

Quick!'

They picked up the pace. The road dipped down a gentle hill. The elephant picked up speed. A man standing outside a pub nearly dropped his phone in amazement as they hurtled past. With a bit of force behind it, the elephant moved through the night as though it were running along by itself. It was almost impossible to steer, though. It careered around corners and veered towards walls; it took all Kirsty's strength to push it back on course. She was panting heavily with the effort, inhaling great lungfuls of dust and grime from its skin. She could hear Dawn and Ben struggling too.

Chug, chug, chug. There was a new noise thumping through the dark skies.

'What's that?' Kirsty asked, looking around.

'Uh-oh,' Ben said. 'That is a helicopter. A police helicopter. They're looking for us. We have to get under cover.'

'They won't be able to see us,' Dawn said. 'It's too dark.'

Suddenly, a beam of white light shone down from the sky behind them. A searchlight, stretching from the helicopter down to the museum. The light hovered for a moment and then started tracing circles along the ground – a larger and larger spiral as the search spread wider. Somewhere nearby a drunk person yelled something rude at the helicopter.

'Move!' Kirsty yelled.

They were sprinting now, pushing as hard as they could, speeding away from the police search behind them. They couldn't hope to stay hidden. Under a searchlight the elephant would be an obvious shaking mass of stolen animal. They needed darkness. Proper darkness.

'The park!' Kirsty said and threw her weight on to the elephant's left leg, steering them away from the road and towards the park. The river meandered through the centre like a black snake. There were no street lights there, only open grass and small clumps of trees. And, best of all, if you followed the river past the boathouses and old trees you would get to the warehouses, and if you went past the warehouses you would get to the Jubilee Street allotments.

They pushed the elephant through the ornate park gates. The skateboards moved more easily over the wide tarmac path. It was as though the elephant was happier in the park, rolling faster as if it could sense the grass and trees and water around them. Perhaps it was reminded of home after all those years indoors.

The throb of the helicopter was further away now, still hovering over the streets and buildings.

The path ahead was dark. The only light came from the stars, cold and high above.

Then, between gasps, Dawn spoke. 'We have to get to the allotment. It won't be long before they find us. It was hardly the most subtle robbery in the world. They'll be coming. They have to know why we're doing this, otherwise there'll be no point to any of it. We'll just be arrested and that will be that.'

'Dawn's right,' Ben agreed. 'We have to go down fighting. We have to get there and make a last stand. You know, like the Alamo.'

'Never heard of it,' Kirsty said.

'Or the Charge of the Light Brigade.'

'Nope.'

'OK. Try to imagine something pointless but heroic.'

'Oh, I see. Fine, let's go.'

And despite their burning lungs and aching arms and the fear of the police helicopter buzzing like a hornet in the sky, they all pushed ahead harder.

Kirsty's legs felt like unwieldy lumps of stone by the time they reached the warehouses. And when they reached the turning for the allotments, her arms were like sacks of wet sand. She was so tired! But she had to keep moving, for Grandad, for Dad and for Ben and Dawn too. She couldn't give in now.

Out of the park, they moved through damp, mossy alleyways. The houses on either side were all dark. An occasional security light winked on as they passed and a few cats hissed in the darkness, but no one woke up. The elephant was a tight fit in the final alleyway, the coarse skin of its flanks just skimming the glistening brick walls as they trundled through. Then the path opened out again and the allotments were before them.

'We have to go to the big gate,' Kirsty said. 'Where the trucks get in.'

They followed the wire fence as far as the gate. Together, they managed to heave them open.

'Shush!' Ben said suddenly. The sound of the helicopter's blades slicing through the night sky was louder. It was definitely coming closer.

'Get inside, now!' Kirsty hissed. With one final heave, they rolled the elephant on to the track. It slowed to a halt just next to grandad's painted shed.

'How can we hide it?' Ben said. 'Is there anything in the shed?'

'We don't want to hide it,' Kirsty said.

'We don't?' Dawn was gasping, barely able to speak after the effort of pushing an elephant for nearly three miles cross-country.

'No. We're making a statement, aren't we? Letting Mr Thomas know that we won't be ignored? How can we do that if no one knows what we've done? Stands to reason. I've made something. Wait here.'

Kirsty disappeared into the shed. They could hear banging as she looked around in the darkness. Then she re-emerged.

'Ta-da!' Kirsty held up the edge of a white sheet that looked more grey in the moonlight. Ben took the opposite edge and stepped back. There was writing on the sheet in dark paint.

'"The elephant for our allotment Mister Thomas!"' Ben read. 'The letters aren't very straight.'

'Well, the sheet was bigger than the shed. It was very hard to paint right,' Kirsty said. 'It says what we want it to say, doesn't it?'

'Hang on,' Ben said. 'Is it me, or can anyone hear two helicopters now?'

Kirsty lowered the sheet and listened. Ben was right. The slow throb of two sets of blades, coming from different directions, cut up the night sky. 'I didn't know that the local police had two helicopters. Actually, I didn't even know they had one helicopter,' she said.

'I don't think it is the police,' Dawn said. 'Looks like Mum's going to get her media campaign after all.' She pointed upwards.

A small helicopter had banked up from the south side of the town. The on-board lights lit up a logo painted on the bottom of the fuselage – 'Atmo News Channel' in its familiar chunky font.

'Oh no,' Ben said. 'We're going to be on the news.'

'It's not "oh no", it's brilliant! This is a great way for Mr Thomas to see our message. Come on, quick – let's put the sheet over the elephant, so they can read it.'

Kirsty jumped up, throwing the sheet above her as though she were making a massive bed. Dawn and Ben hurried to help, tweaking and tugging the sheet into place. When they had finished it looked like the elephant was wearing a huge saddle blanket.

The Atmo helicopter swept across the allotments. It didn't have doors, so they could see a cameraman leaning out, desperate to be the first to capture the news story. The helicopter circled again, lower down. Someone switched on a searchlight that locked on to the colossal shape of the elephant. Kirsty heard whoops of joy coming from the sky above them.

It felt for a moment as though time had stopped, that the elephant was held in the searchlight by a powerful force and that everything around it was frozen too. Dawn, Ben, the elephant, the shed – everything caught in a steady beam of light.

Then the night suddenly became bedlam. Sirens rang out all around. Police cars roared up to the allotment site. The helicopters circled overhead. Lights came on in the houses nearby and the first trickle of people opened their curtains, then their doors, to get a better view.

'Blimey!' Kirsty whispered.

Officers in black uniforms slipped out of the squad cars; police formed a cordon around the perimeter fence. Some crouched down behind their cars, others stood calmly, waiting for instructions.

'I think we might be busted,' Dawn said.

'Really? You think?' There was a high note in Ben's voice, like the beginning of hysteria. Kirsty reached out her hand and rested it on his shoulder. She gave a little squeeze.

Ben turned to her. In the harsh beam of the search-lights, his eyes seemed wild, his jaw loose somehow. And then Kirsty saw something change as he looked at her. His mouth closed firmly, his eyebrows furrowed. Kirsty realised that Ben was trying his absolute hardest to be brave. And he was managing it!

'Don't worry,' he said. 'I know it's going to be all right.' Then he stepped away from them and started waving his arms above his head to attract attention. He yelled at the police officers, 'Listen up. We've got the museum's elephant. It's ours now. And if you don't do what we ask, we'll . . . we'll kick it! It's hollow, you know! We'll kick it and then it will be ruined! No use to anyone. So you'd better listen!'

There was a moment of silence. Then an officer in a peaked hat brought a loudspeaker up to his lips. 'OK, son. No need to be hasty. We'll send in a hostage liaison officer to talk to you. You can tell her what this is all about, OK?'

'No. All we want is for Mr Thomas at the council to give this allotment to my sister. That's it.'

'I don't think I heard you right, son. Did you just say you've burgled the museum so that your sister can grow lettuces?'

'That's right! So you need to get Mr Thomas down here right now!'

Kirsty and Dawn both stared at Ben in amazement. He smiled at them, a huge, contented smile that seemed to stretch his face wide open. 'They're sending in a hostage liaison officer!' he said. 'We've got a hostage! How cool is that!'

'Ben, are you all right?' Kirsty asked. He was grinning at the circle of police as though they were long-lost friends.

'I'm fine! This is great!'

'This is a stand-off, right?' Dawn asked.

'Yup.'

'So, all we have to do is wait until Mr Thomas gets here?'

'I suppose.'

'Well, then. I'm going to sit down. It could be ages. Come on, let's get comfy. I brought some food for you. I thought you'd be hungry,' Dawn said.

Dawn pulled Kirsty and Ben down into the dark space underneath the elephant. There was enough room for the three of them to sit quite comfortably. Dawn opened her bag and pulled out a sandwich box. Kirsty tugged off the lid and began chewing at the cheese butties, her cheeks puffed out like a hamster. Dawn also pulled out her make-up bag.

'What you messing with that for?' Ben asked.

'We're going to be on the news, aren't we? In front of the TV cameras? Well, I'm going to look fabulous for it.'

'TV?' Kirsty stopped chewing and stared at Dawn with a grin. 'Do you really think we'll be on TV?'

'Hey, look!' Ben said. He pointed over to where the officer with the loudspeaker stood. Kirsty peered out from under the elephant. There, behind the police cars, was Mum storming up to the site. And Dad was with her! Neither were dressed properly. Mum just had a dressing gown tied around her. Dad had at least pulled on some jeans, but he was walking in his slippers across the path.

Kirsty felt Ben reach for her hand. She squeezed

tight. 'He's out of bed,' she said. 'And he looks pretty interested in what's going on.' It suddenly felt like there was nothing else that mattered. The police, the helicopters – it all seemed to fade into the background. The noise and the lights and the action were not important any more. Dad was here.

'Oh no, look!' Dawn said. She pointed in the other direction. Angela was forcing her way through the crowd. She was fully dressed and groomed, her make-up done perfectly. She'd been thinking of the telly too, Kirsty thought. Angela was smiling and waving at Dad. Dad half-raised his hand back. Angela reached the car where Mum and Dad stood. They were talking, but Kirsty was too far away to hear their conversation.

'What do you suppose they're saying?' Kirsty asked.

'Oh, you know. A lifetime's grounding. Shut in our rooms till we're old enough to vote. Bread and water for every meal till Doomsday.' Ben shrugged and bit into a chocolate bar that he'd found in the sandwich box.

'Do you really think so?'

Dawn was silent for a moment. Then she sighed deeply. 'I think they're doing their best to get us out of trouble with the police. They love us, don't they?'

'Dad looks quite angry now,' Kirsty said, reaching for another cheese sandwich.

Dawn peered out from behind the elephant's leg. Dad was slapping the bumper of a police car. Someone had given Mum a mug of tea.

'Any sign of the council yet?' Ben asked.

Suddenly the loudspeaker crackled into life. 'This is impossible!' a voice blustered. Kirsty looked out. It was Mr Thomas. He was here. He walked forwards, his slippers flapping as he climbed over a row of leeks. 'This is ridiculous!' he bellowed. 'Preposterous! I've been woken up in the middle of the night! So has Mrs Thomas! And for what? An escaped elephant ransomed by some cheeky monkeys!'

'Does he mean us?'

'Yup.'

Mr Thomas was closer now and still yelling.

'We have to give him our demands,' Ben said. 'Do you want me to do it?'

'No. I'll do it,' Kirsty said. 'But it would be nice if you'd stand near me, both of you.'

Kirsty stepped out. Ben and Dawn followed and stood right beside her. She took a deep breath. 'Mr Thomas,' she said. 'Mum, Dad. Everyone. We took the elephant for a reason. Not just for fun. Although it was fun. We want to keep Grandad's allotment. We want you all to listen to us. Especially Dad. Dad, we love you and we want you back. That's all.'

246

Mr Thomas stopped walking. The loudspeaker hung down by his side. A ripple ran through the police officers as Kirsty spoke. Dad sat down on the bonnet of the car. Would they listen? Would they understand?

And then, Mr Thomas began to chuckle – slowly at first, but then louder and louder until he was clutching his sides and crying. 'They stole a ruddy elephant! A great, big elephant!' he gasped.

Dad gasped. 'They ruddy did too!' Dad stood shakily and walked out towards them. He held open his arms. He looked so thin and pale in the glow of the searchlight. Kirsty ran forward. Dad scooped her into the air and held her close. She could feel the rough growth of his beard against her cheek as she hugged him back.

'I'm sorry,' he whispered.

Kirsty could hear Mr Thomas still giggling to himself as she closed her eyes against Dad's shoulder. He carried her back to Ben and Dawn. She could feel them hugging her too. She squeezed Dad as hard as she could.

For the next hour, the police officers scribbled in their pads; Dawn answered questions in front of a few television cameras; Ben snuggled inside a warm blanket, holding a white mug full of hot tea.

Kirsty sat on an upturned bucket as she watched the elephant being driven away on a truck. The sky was getting lighter, the stars winking out one by one like the candles on an old man's birthday cake. The sun would rise soon. She lay her palms down on to the grass and pushed against the earth. What would happen now? To the allotment? To them? The earth was damp and cold from the gathering dew. The allotments were emptying out. Soon there would be no sign that any of this had ever happened.

Kirsty stood up and wiped her wet hands on the front of her shirt, then went to find her family.

WEDNESDAY

CHAPTER 34

The rest of the night was a blur. Angela whisked Dawn and Ben away before Kirsty could even say thank you to them. Kirsty was tucked up in bed with a hot-water bottle as soon as they stepped through the door. She slept without dreaming for hours. She woke around lunchtime, with the sounds of the day creeping in through her open window and a breeze fluttering the curtain. When she finally got out of bed, she could hear voices downstairs. Dad and Mum were talking to someone. A grown-up someone. The police? Kirsty wrapped her dressing gown about her tightly and pulled hard at the belt. She crept downstairs.

She trod carefully down the hall until she reached the living room.

'Oh, you're awake, then?' Mum had seen her. Mr Thomas was sitting on the settee, a cup balanced on a saucer on his knee. He smiled at her. Dad sat next to Mr Thomas. His beard was gone. He was wearing his favourite red T-shirt. Kirsty stared at him. He was out of bed! There was a glowing kind of joy in her stomach that she had never felt before. Even if she ended up in prison after last night, it would be OK, because Dad would be able to come and visit.

Mr Thomas spoke. 'I thought it was a dream! Really, I did. Mrs Thomas set me straight. She said in all her years she had never been woken up by a stuffed elephant before, and it set me laughing all over again.'

'Morning, Mr Thomas,' Kirsty said.

Mum went into the kitchen and came back with a mug of tea. She passed it to Kirsty with a wink. The tea felt nice and warm, and Kirsty was glad of something to hide her face behind.

'Sit down,' Dad said, pointing to the empty armchair. Kirsty lowered herself into it, keeping both hands wrapped around the mug to stop them shaking. 'Am I going to prison?' she blurted out.

Dad looked serious for a moment, then smiled. 'No, not this time. The museum isn't going to press charges. It seems that Mr Thomas is on the board of trustees. Which is not to say that you won't be punished, young lady.'

Kirsty's eyes widened. Was this the lifetime of hard

252

chores that Ben had predicted?

Mr Thomas spoke. 'Yes. We've been talking. We think that a few months' community service is in order.'

Kirsty's heart sank as she thought of the miserable things she had seen on the TV: the toilet cleaning, the wall painting, the stupid overalls they had to wear.

'Yes,' Mr Thomas continued. 'We think it would be a good idea for you to do a spot of work out in the community, helping others. We were thinking you might take over one of the recently vacated allotment plots, thus ensuring the continued vitality and –'

Had she heard right? An allotment plot? Kirsty squealed, put down her mug and ran over to Mr Thomas. She threw her arms around him in a bear hug. Luckily, his cup was empty before it hit the carpet.

'Thank you! Thank you!'

She stepped back and looked at Dad. He smiled, but his eyes still had a far-away look. She reached out and touched his face. 'It's all right, Dad. There's no need to be sad. Everything's going to be better soon.'

Dad smiled. 'I know. But you're so like your grandad. This is what you both wanted. I'm sorry I didn't see it before. I haven't been well. I wasn't paying attention to the good things that I've got. I was too caught up in the bad stuff. But I feel a bit stronger now. Come on.' He stood up. 'We've got work to do down the allotments. Go and get your wellies on.'

'Dad! Brilliant!' Kirsty threw herself into Dad's arms and felt him hug her tight. He was on his way back to them. When he finally let go, Kirsty asked, 'But would you mind if I went by myself? Just for this first time.'

Dad exchanged a look with Mum, as though something was being decided. Then he said, 'Sure. We'll come over later. You can tell us all your plans.'

SUMMER

EPILOGUE

By the time that summer arrived, Kirsty's community service had paid off. She had worked on the allotment all spring and now green shoots had sprouted into towering plants; leaves had unfurled into a lush canopy and, if she was really quiet, she could hear jaguars padding past in the undergrowth.

It was just like she had planned it. Coming here alone the day after they had stolen the elephant, she had stood on the dark earth and made a new promise to Grandad. She had promised that she would always keep the people she loved close to her, no matter how far they might travel. And she'd promised to plant some marrows, even if they did taste revolting.

And she had done it. But it wasn't just her. Dawn and Ben were facing justice too. Every weekend they had come down with forks and hoes and moans and groans to help. Dad came some days too. He didn't get better all in one night. He was still sad sometimes, but he got out of bed every day. Kirsty was sure that he was going to be OK.

One Saturday, Kirsty asked everyone to meet at the allotment. Mum, Dad, Ben and Dawn, even Angela.

The sun burned hot above them, insects buzzed among the flowers. It was a perfect day. They stood in a circle. Dad held a small jar. Grandad's ashes. They had agreed that Kirsty would speak. Now that it was time, she wasn't sure if she could, the lump in her throat was so big. Then she felt her sister squeeze her hand. She stepped forwards. 'Grandad. I know you can hear me. We've all come to say that we love you. And we miss you. And we hope you think we're taking good care of your allotment.'

Kirsty saw Mum wipe her eyes with a tissue. Then Dad stepped forwards. He moved up to the tallest sunflower. He knelt down and unscrewed the jar. A small cloud of dust billowed out. He lifted the urn and shook it on to the ground. The light grey ash swirled for a moment and then settled over the brown earth.

No one spoke. The sun twinkled on the yellow petals of the flower. Then Dad smiled at Kirsty. 'I put some paint in the shed. I thought we could redecorate it today.'

Kirsty looked at the shed, at Grandad's yin-yang and her dolphins. Redecorate? No way! 'Dad, we can't paint over the dolphins.'

Dad smiled. 'No,' he said. 'But we can add to them. There are the other walls to do. Mum and I were thinking that an elephant might look great on one of those. What do you think?'

Kirsty grinned. 'Brilliant,' she said.

ACKNOWLEDGEMENTS

I have to start by saying thank you to Kirsty Jenkins. She'd be very cross otherwise! When I read her story in the paper, I just knew I wanted to write about it. She gave me lots of great interviews and advice about gardening. I hope Kirsty likes the way I told her story. She told me she'll be keeping a blog for a while when the book comes out, so I guess I'll find out! You can read it at **www.kirstyjenkins.blogspot.com**.

I also have to thank Rosemary, Emma and Julia, as well as Alex D., Alex H., Janine, Jim, Liz, Matt and Sue.

ABOUT THE AUTHOR

Elen Caldecott recently graduated with an MA in Writing for Young People from Bath Spa University.

Before becoming a writer, she was an archaeologist, a nurse, a theatre usher and a museum security guard. It was while working at the museum that Elen realised there is a way to steal anything if you think about it hard enough. Elen either had to become a master thief, or create some characters to do it for her – and so she began her debut novel, *How Kirsty Jenkins Stole the Elephant*.

Elen lives in Bristol with her husband, Simon, and one day – when they live in a bigger flat – they will be joined by a dog.